# Comanche Gap

## A Lone Rider Novel, #2

### Rusty Beauquet

**Six-Gun Western Heritage Press**

# Contents

# Chapter One

## The Law Don't Go Around Here

COMANCHE GAP WASN'T THE roughest town west of the Pecos, but was trying hard to earn the distinction.

Named for a great mesa formed of 135 million-year-old limestone deposits and subsequently split by erosion to provide a natural gateway through the Castle Mountains, the town was born as a weigh station for the Butterfield Overland Mail stage line. Twice a week, stagecoaches stopped at Comanche Gap on their 2,795-mile, twenty-five-day overland treks between Tipton, Missouri and San Francisco, California, while transiting the town's namesake pass.

Indian nomads seeking buffalo on the plateau bordered by the Colorado River to the east and the Pecos River to the west or salt from a natural salt deposit near a lake on a land grant from Mexico to a man named Juan Cordova had used Comanche Gap proper as a gateway since prehistoric times. Spanish explorer Álvar Núñez Cabeza de Vaca passed through the mile-long break in 1535. With the advent of the Comanche war trail by 1800, Comanches, Kiowas, Rocky Mountain Utes, and plains Apaches used Comanche Gap to travel to and from their raiding grounds in Mexico.

In more contemporary times, William A. Peril drove the first cattle herd of any size through Comanche Gap in 1864 en route from San Antonio to Chihuahua. However, the most noteworthy cattle drive occurred in 1866, when Charles Goodnight, Oliver Loving, and eighteen men trailed 2,000 longhorn steers and breeding cows to Fort Sumner, New Mexico, from the Brazos in northern Texas through Comanche Gap. The first stage traversed the pass on September 25, 1858.

The Butterfield line constructed a two-story stage station of native limestone at the gap's west end, where a spring supplied the needs of attendants and stage teams. Then, as the outpost grew into the town of Comanche Gap, other buildings of unexceptional architecture, perched haphazardly on the rugged slopes of Castle Mountain to the north and the King Mountain to the south, sprang up. Besides the Butterfield station, the town boasted a livery stable, mercantile, cantina, and boarding house.

The cantina and boarding house both occupied adobe structures, once part of a defunct cattle ranch, with the latter occupying the larger building that once served as the ranch house. Since the stage station didn't serve food, passengers took their meals with other travelers at the boarding house. The inhabitants of Comanche Gap, which fluctuated between one hundred ten and one hundred sixty souls, lived in a collection of weather-beaten shacks and nondescript hovels constructed of whatever materials were at hand when the original occupants built the shelters.

Comanche Gap's hopes of attaining the reputation as the roughest town west of the Pecos rested primarily upon its significant outlaw population, of which the town was secretly just a little proud. As a result, it wasn't uncommon to witness a sudden thunder of galloping hooves on the town's main street several times a week that scattered indignant, squawking chickens and startled, dodging townsfolk as one or more outlaws raced out of town and through the gap. Before the dust had settled, a posse most usually appeared. Yet rarely did the lawmen pursue the outlaws through the gap that led to sixty-two miles of desert badlands without reliable water holes. Instead, knowing further pursuit was probably futile, the posse more often than not dismounted at the cantina and bellied up to the bar for a drink or two before heading back the way they had come.

The town of Comanche Gap didn't have two things. There was no town jail or a lawman. The town's inhabitants saddled their own broncs when settling disputes among themselves, usually through the liberal use of knives or six guns as mediators. As many an inhabitant often told outsiders: "The law don't go around here."

No posse followed the lone rider on the long-legged roan, and he rode easy rather than at a gallop when he entered Comanche Gap shortly before noon as the sun climbed higher in the brazen sky. The higher it got, the hotter it got. The heat dried the rider's perspiration before he felt the moisture. He wondered if it got any hotter whether the heat would explode the cartridges in the loops on his gun belt. The rider was a tall, gray-eyed man, broad of shoulders and chest. He wore a black, high-crowned hat, black cotton shirt, and worn stovepipe chaps over black wool pants. He carried a worn, tied-down Colt with bone grips on his right hip, and there was a Model 1866 brass-framed .44 rimfire Henry rifle in his saddle holster.

The man rode first to the livery to stable his horse. Then, and only after first seeing to the care of his horse, did he cross the street to the cantina. Well acquainted with the country west of the Pecos, the man knew the reputation of the town. So when he entered, he surveyed the room with the glance of a careful man. Then he took in the bartender with another before allowing his eyes to rest on the only man standing at the bar. Aware of the stranger's eyes upon him, the man, Joe Merritt, felt a prickly sensation at the nape of his neck. The newcomer crossed the plank floor to the bar and ordered a whiskey.

After downing the shot, the man winced and set the glass back on the bar.

"Will you have another drink?" asked Walt Hansen, the red-haired, smooth-faced bartender.

The stranger grimaced. "No, I've never been much for drinking turpentine."

Walt chuckled. "It's varnish, friend, not turpentine. Coffin Varnish. We distill it out back from only the choicest ingredients. But, yeah, she's a little green, and the first couple goes down a little rough. But Coffin Varnish sure does the job for drinkin' men."

"I'm inclined to agree with you if going plumb blind is what you're aiming for."

The barman shot him a look of irritation. The stranger ignored the look and jerked his head toward the street outside the front door.

"Is that boarding house down the street a good place to eat?"

"If you're not as particular about what you eat as what you drink. It's plain fare, but the best around here since Harry's Boarding House is the only eatin' place in town. But it's good grub that sticks to a man's ribs."

Walt watched the newcomer, noting the strongly drawn face and the faint weather lines around his intelligent gray eyes. But something beneath the man's quiet demeanor warned an observant man to tread lightly around him. Walt, if nothing else, was an observant man.

Conscious of Walt Hansen's attention, the stranger rested his eyes on the barkeep, measuring him again.

"What's in Comanche Gap?" he asked suddenly.

Joe Merritt looked over at the man and replied before the bartender could. "A few dozen shacks, a couple of adobes, including this cantina. Then there's the stage station up the hill at the gap's west end."

"How many men?"

"Maybe eighty. Maybe a hundred and twenty." Merritt allowed himself a toothy grin. "She fluctuates right sudden at times."

"Who's the big man in these parts?"

"Otto Schmidt, if you mean who owns this place. Tom Hale, if you mean who runs it." Merritt added gently, "Hale is hell on wheels with a gun. As good as Ben Thompson, maybe, or Allison."

The man nodded. "I'm looking for a man of about twenty named Blair Ward. He's riding a buckskin gelding with a Flying X brand. You see him come through here?"

"You a law dog, mister? Walt Hansen asked with a hard look. "Cause the law don't go around here."

"I said I was looking for him, not huntin' him."

"That's good," Hansen said. "Cause the law don't go around here."

"Yeah, you said that already. So, have you seen him or not?"

"I don't recollect seeing anyone answering the description."

Merritt turned away when the newcomer asked his question and occupied himself with intently studying his empty glass.

A shadow of a smile appeared on the stranger's lips. "Thanks," he said, tossing a coin on the bar. Then he crossed the room to the door and went out. After looking left and right, he crossed the street and made for the boarding house.

Merritt looked up at Hansen. "Now, who would that be?" he asked. "He's somebody, and you know them all, Walt."

"Not him," Hansen said with a puzzled look. "Although there's something about him that seems mighty familiar."

"He's not runnin' from the law," Merritt said firmly. "He's on the hunt."

"No," Hansen said thoughtfully. "He ain't runnin'. That's for sure."

# Chapter Two

## A Confrontation

THE STRANGER CROSSED THE wide, unpainted, and unpeopled porch that was too hot for idlers and pushed the door open, walking into the dining room in the front. It was a long room containing two oilcloth-covered tables, each with benches along the sides. Two women and a man sat at a table, the women with some space between them, and the man sat facing each other. The older but not unattractive woman wore a yellow dress and heavy makeup. She glanced at the stranger when he walked in, then looked with renewed interest and curiosity a second time. The younger woman was tall and of slight build, with brown eyes and raven hair, made to seem even darker because of her fair, light brown skin. She wore a riding habit—a short black jacket spangled with silver over a white shirt, black breeches, and tall black boots. A black flat-crowned hat lay on the bench beside her. The stranger found the woman undeniably more than attractive. As he admired her uncommon beauty, the woman talked with the well-dressed man who smoked a cigar. Suddenly, he found he wanted to know her.

The newcomer took a seat at the second table facing the door and removed his hat. The older woman got up and brought over a tray with a plate of food on it.

"It's beans today if you're looking for grub," she said.

"That suits me. I'm hungry, and I'll eat anything you've got that won't bite back."

The woman grinned and lifted the plate from the tray and set it on the table before him—brown beans and sliced onions and jalapenos on the side with cornbread.

"Riding through?" the woman asked.

"No," the man said shortly, but then he smiled to soften the brevity and stiffness of his speech. "I'm as far as I go for a spell. Besides the grub, I'd like a bed and bath."

The woman smiled. "I'm Harriet Fisher. My friends call me Harry, and I run the place. Beds are seventy-five cents a night with breakfast and supper included or five dollars by the week."

The man gave her another quick measuring glance. "I'll take it a night at a time. Not sure how long I'm staying."

"Not much here if you're looking for work. Comanche Gap isn't like other places."

"I'm not huntin' a job."

"Where you from, cowboy?"

"Out Fort Stockton way."

"Are you a cattleman?"

"Might be."

The man at the other table stood. "Then I'll see you tomorrow, Miss Espinosa."

"Yes, my vaqueros and I will arrive at your rancho by noon, Señor Logan."

The stranger shifted his eyes from Fisher to the man. "You're Frank Logan?" he said. There was an edge to his voice, and Harry Fisher moved hastily aside. Having worked in saloons from Dodge City to Fort Worth for a time, she recognized it when she saw trouble brewing.

Logan also noticed the tone of the man's voice and frowned. "That's my name," he said. "Have we met, friend?"

Ignoring the question, the stranger said soberly, "I'm here to cut your herd. I hear you've got some branded Flying X stock running with your cattle."

Surprised and angry in equal measure, Logan removed the cigar from his mouth, his face flushed. Logan, a strongly made man with a square face, was unaccustomed to a man speaking to him in such an insolent manner.

"You're misinformed, stranger," he said. "If there are any cattle with such a brand in this country, and I doubt it, I'm unaware of it. There are certainly none on my range. Furthermore, no one is cutting my herd."

The stranger stood up, pulled a folded document from his pocket, and put it on the table in front of Logan.

"That's my authority, Mr. Logan. I'm an agent of the Flying X Ranch, fully authorized by the owner, Colonel Alfred Ward, to find and take possession of his property. He's lost over a thousand head from his spread over at Fort Stockton. And he wants them back."

"If he's lost cattle, there over the border by now."

"I'll be along directly to cut that herd," the stranger said, his tone now icy cold.

The raven-haired young woman stared at him with a shocked and concerned expression that annoyed Logan.

"There is no need for concern, Miss Espinosa," Logan said soothingly. "Someone has misinformed this man, that's all." Then, turning back to the newcomer, he said, "You stay off my ranch. I've no cattle but my own. I don't care what authority you claim." Logan waved dismissively at the document on the table that he had not bothered to inspect. "You stay off my ranch. Is that clear?"

"I'll be along," the man persisted, his voice still cool. "You can count on it, Logan." The man picked up a hunk of cornbread from his plate and took a bite. After chewing, he said, "And while I'm there, I'll ask a question or two. First, I'll want to know what happened to Blair Ward, who rode over this way two weeks ago looking for that Flying X stock."

Logan's lips became a hard line. He glanced at the young woman with whom he had talked and saw the concern now deeply etched on her face. She was looking at the stranger. Then he glanced back at the newcomer.

"I know nothing about any Blair Ward," he retorted. "I've never heard the name."

"I hope you know nothing about him," the man said, taking another bite of the cornbread. "Colonel Ward is a friend of mine, and Blair is his only son. I also hope you have none of his cattle. And you won't object to me cutting your herd if you're wise. That might go a long way toward peaceably settling the matter."

"I do object, so save yourself the ride. You set foot on my ranch, and I'll throw you off."

The girl named Espinosa spoke up. "Señor Logan, my father, Don Pablo, will want a clear title to the cattle you're selling us. I want this man to cut the herd before

I'll accept delivery and pay you. We want no trouble later."

His face a mask of undisguised rage, Logan snatched the cigar from his lips, intending to reply. But overcome with anger, he stopped himself. What kind of foolishness was this? He and the woman had already agreed. He would sell her father fifteen hundred head of cattle for eighteen dollars a head. Now this saddle tramp had butted in and threatened to spoil the deal. Who did the man think he was? Didn't he know he was fooling about with Frank Logan?

"Your title will be clean," Logan said to the woman sharply. Then he turned to the stranger. "What's your name?" he demanded.

The stranger pinned Logan with a withering stare, his gray eyes appearing almost black. Yet his tanned face with the weathered lines about the eyes revealed no emotion.

"I'm Ian Murphy," he said tonelessly.

Logan paled, looking as if the man had struck him. Ian Murphy, the gunfighter whose name became a legend in the cattle towns throughout the west? Men mentioned his name in the same breath as Allison, Hardin, and Hitchcock. Logan had heard Murphy sometimes worked as a ranch foreman and sometimes as a mere ranch hand or drover on the cattle trails to New Mexico Territory, Colorado, and Kansas. Rumors said he was a mysterious man who maintained an unassuming demeanor rather than hunting trouble and often went by other names. Then, suddenly, when provoked, he would step from the shadows. Then, after his Colt roared for an instant, spelling death for the unfortunate fool who had goaded him, Murphy would disappear into the shadows again.

Logan spoke, but choked on the words. So he turned, hurried to the door, went out, and slammed it behind him. Before he reached the street, sweat had drenched his shirt. He stopped to mop his face with a bandana. Murphy, here in Comanche Gap! And with questions about Flying X stock and Blair Ward. Those cattle were part of the stock he intended to sell to Espinosa. Now she demanded that he permit the cut. What would he do? What could he do?

# Chapter Three
## The Surprising Señorita

After watching Logan depart, Murphy laid some coins on the table and smiled at Harry Fisher.

"Mighty good grub," he said, putting on his hat. "Sure beats my campfire cooking."

"Thank you," Fisher beamed. "Would you care to see your room now?"

"Later," Murphy said. "I want to look the country over and get the lay of the land. I'll be back before sundown."

"As you wish."

"Pardon me, Señor Murphy," the younger woman said. "I am Maria Espinosa Díaz."

"It's me who begs your pardon, Señorita Espinosa," Murphy said, tipping his hat. "I apologize for causing you any discomfort and hope I didn't spoil your lunch."

Espinosa smiled. "Your apology is unnecessary. Is it your opinion that Señor Logan is a cattle thief?"

"My information is that Logan doesn't steal cattle himself, but that he isn't too particular about what brand cattle wear he buys or the people selling them as long as the price is right."

"So you suspect he has stolen cattle in his herd?"

"I suspect it but won't know for sure until I cut his herd."

"Understood. I wish to accompany you when you inspect Señor Logan's cattle."

"As much as I'd enjoy the company, Señorita Espinosa, that isn't possible. You heard what Logan said about running me off his spread if I showed up. And I expect he might try. So, I couldn't guarantee your safety."

"Guaranteeing my safety is not your responsibility, Señor. I'm perfectly capable of taking care of myself. I must determine if there is truth to your accusation, as my father, Don Pablo Espinosa, does not trade in stolen cattle."

"All right then," Murphy said. "But I'm riding out to Logan's spread right now. I don't want to give him time to move his herd."

"Very well," Espinosa said. "My horse is at the livery stable."

"Please allow me to fetch your horse, then. Mine is at the livery too, so I'll bring your horse along back here when I collect mine."

"Very well, thank you for the courtesy."

Murphy tipped his hat again. "Thank you for insisting on the cut." Then he went out.

⁓

Maria Espinosa glanced curiously after Murphy as he walked out of the dining room. What was it about the name Ian Murphy that could shock a man such as Frank Logan? The rancher was, and she knew, a man of some influence in Comanche Gap. People respected him, yet a mere name had shocked him speechless. The name had not only shocked Logan, but had frightened him. The fear she saw in the man's face was palatable.

Espinosa glanced at Harriet Fisher, who was still staring thoughtfully at the door Murphy had walked out through. Espinosa started to speak, but hesitated. She knew Fisher had worked as a dance hall girl before establishing the Comanche Gap boarding house. It wasn't considered proper to consort with such women. But her curiosity got the best of her.

"Do you know of this man, Ian Murphy?" she said to Fisher.

"I saw him once before," Fisher said with a sigh. "It was up in Dodge City years ago. But even then, he was wonderful, though a little strange."

"But why did the name frighten Señor Logan so?" Espinosa said. Fisher's obvious admiration of the man annoyed her. "I don't understand?"

"Because he's Ian Murphy," Fisher exclaimed. "Don't tell me you've never heard of him. He's a gunfighter, one of the fastest men alive, and one of the deadliest." Fisher looked thoughtful.

"Yet I suppose that's only part of it. You never see Murphy around like you do the others—Bat Masterson, Luke Short, Ben Thompson. You always see them around in the cattle towns. But Murphy comes, and he goes. No one might see him for months on end or for a year or more. And when they do, most folks never dream that it's him, the infamous Ian Murphy until trouble comes around."

"It all sounds quite fantastic and absurd," Espinosa said. "I don't understand all the excitement over a common killer. Back in Fort Sumner, the authorities would put him in jail, and that would be the end of it."

Fisher turned angrily on the young woman. "You aren't in New Mexico Territory now! And Ian Murphy never killed a man who didn't have it coming."

"But he's only a gunman."

"A gunfighter," Fisher corrected. "Maybe he hasn't always been on the side of the law. But he has always been on the side of fair play."

"I'm afraid it's all beyond me," Espinosa said sharply. "Gunman and gunfighter are two words with the same meaning. But thank you for the information. At least now I know who I'm dealing with."

Espinosa got to her feet, went out the door, and closed it behind her.

"Well!" Fisher exclaimed in exasperation. "Isn't she the snobby one?"

⁂

MARIA ESPINOSA PAUSED OUTSIDE on the porch to await Murphy's arrival with her horse. It was strange to find herself in this sun-blistered little town about to ride into the countryside with an infamous gunman. Yet how else could she accomplish what her father had sent her to do? She thought for a moment about insisting to Murphy that they first stop at the camp of her vaqueros. Perhaps it would be wise to have Antonio, her segundo, accompany them to Logan's rancho. But she dismissed the idea. She had to prove to her father and the vaqueros with this trip that she was competent to run the affairs of their rancho back in Fort Sumner.

Unfortunately, fate had not seen fit to bless Don Pablo Espinosa with sons. Her mother, Sonsoles, had perished after giving birth to Maria, and her father had raised her as if she were the son he would never have. Now that he was growing old, it fell to Maria to run things at the rancho on a day-to-day basis. As badly as they needed the cattle to fulfill her father's contracts with the government, Maria knew she would bring shame to him if she returned home with stolen cattle. That would undo the trust she had painstakingly built with her father about her competency.

Maria wanted nothing more than to complete her task quickly and return home with the cattle to the land she loved, with its towering mesas, endless stretches of desert that looked purple in the distance, the arroyos, and yes, even the abundant cacti. The hacienda itself that her father had built was a dream. Standing on its wide verandahs, she could look in all directions for fifty miles over the land she would one day own and control. All of it produced a charm she missed, especially now as she stood in this small weather-beaten Texas town filled with bandits and gunmen.

Murphy appeared from around the corner, leading the horses. Suddenly, she regretted not asking Fisher more questions. Was this Murphy honest? Could she trust him? Since she began running the business of the rancho, everyone she met had treated her with respect and courtesy. If it surprised men to see a woman buying and selling cattle and horses, none had shown it. And until now, no one had tried to take advantage of her. Yet this man Murphy had accused Logan of trying to sell her stolen cattle. Was it true? Or was it Murphy who hoped to take advantage of a woman?

Watching him approach, the way Murphy walked, surprised Maria. He moved more like a woodsman or the Indios that inhabited the reservation next to Fort Sumner than the American cowboys she had encountered.

"Here's your horse, Señorita," Murphy said, handing her the reins of the pinto that had a coat with large patches of white mixed with brown. "He's a good-looking animal."

"Yes, he is a fine horse," Maria agreed. She opened a saddlebag, withdrew a black leather gun belt inlaid with silver conchos, and belted it around her diminutive waist.

Murphy saw there was a shiny, silver Colt in the holster. It looked like one of the newer double-action models Colt had begun producing a few years back. Murphy had seen women carry guns before, but mostly small ones easy to conceal somewhere, not on their hips as this young woman did. But he did not remark.

The unlikely pair mounted their horses and headed out of town.

# Chapter Four

## The Rustlers

FIVE MEN SAT TOGETHER in the shade of a mesquite thicket around a dead campfire with a tinned iron coffee pot blackened by smoke suspended above it. A boot scraped on gravel and a tin cup clanked against a rock. A sixth man squatted at the edge of the thicket, looking out into the distance, watching an approaching black speck that eventually grew into a horse and a rider that became Frank Logan on his bay gelding.

The squatting man, Baldwin Ren, stood up, putting his hands at the small of his back and arching against the stiffness. He was a big man, wide of shoulder and girth. Ren walked out to meet Logan.

Logan swung down from the saddle. His face darkened into a scowl, and his eyes flashed angrily.

"When you sold me those cattle, you swore there would be no trouble," Logan said. "Well, we've got trouble. Or, I should say, more trouble."

"What trouble? More Flying X riders in town?"

"One rider," Logan said. "And in this case, one is God's plenty. Ian Murphy is in town asking questions about Flying X stock and that Ward kid. And he claims to speak for that Fort Stockton rancher."

"Ian Murphy?" Ren said, scratching his unshaven chin. "The gunman?"

"Yes, that Ian Murphy. He braced me at the boarding house in town and said he's coming out here to cut the herd."

Ren glanced back over his shoulder at the mesquite thicket and then at Logan.

"Well, if he shows up out here, Ian Murphy or no, it will be six guns against one. He won't cut the herd. Besides, he can't prove nothin', Logan. We've already changed the Flying X brands to your Double Diamond. How about the Mexican woman? Is she ready to take delivery?"

"We were arranging that when Murphy butted into the conversation. She sided with him and said she won't take delivery unless Murphy cuts the herd."

"Well, it appears to me we'll have to handle Murphy the same way we handled the Ward kid and his four cowboys. But it will cost you extra this time. Ian Murphy is a right dangerous man."

"I don't care what it costs as long as Tom Hale removes the problem. And this time, you're paying him. Also, I'm not standing any loss on that cattle. If the deal falls through, I expect you to give me back the money I paid you."

"Hold your horses, Logan. There ain't no reason to get excited. Tom will take care of Murphy, and the problem gets solved. I never expected that fella at Fort Stockton would even miss those beeves before you got them sold and on the way to New Mexico Territory."

"So, you'll speak to Hale and make the arrangements?"

"Why, sure. Soon as I get the chance. But I reckon I better stick here until Murphy shows up."

Logan stroked his chin. "You and the boys could take care of him when he gets here," he said. "Then we wouldn't have to involve Hale."

Ren shook his head. "Me and the boys get along alright, but we're not gun slicks. Not in the class of an Ian Murphy, anyway. Sure, we could take him, but some of us would likely get shot. So we best let Tom handle it."

"Then you better send someone into town after him now," Logan said. "Murphy seems determined to cut the herd, and when you tell him no, he may give you a fight whether you want it or don't."

"When do you expect he plans to cut the herd?"

"He may be on his way here now for all I know. That's why I came directly here from town. The woman intended to take delivery tomorrow at noon. So, I expect Murphy to show sooner rather than later."

"Alright, then. I better keep everyone here. We'll have to do the best we can to turn him away and hope Murphy isn't crazy enough to start something with six-to-one odds against him. Then Tom can tackle him when he gets back to town."

"Do whatever you think best, Ren. Just solve the problem so we can deliver the cattle. Preferably tomorrow noon."

Logan turned, mounted the bay, and rode away.

"What's eatin' Logan?" Zeke Newell said, sidling up beside Ren. "He looked fit to be roped and tied."

"That Fort Stockton rancher sent Ian Murphy to look for his cows this time. Seems Murphy braced Logan back in town and said he was coming out here to cut the herd."

"Ian Murphy?" Newell blurted. "That man's a sure enough killer."

"Yeah, I've heard of him. But if he shows up, we've got to keep him away from the herd. He may think a Double Diamond brand is a little too convenient when he's looking for cows wearing a Flying X. Come on. We need to tell the others what to expect."

Back at the mesquite grove, Ren shared the information Logan had given him. The expression on old Burt McMullin's face was something to see. McMullin's eyes were wide open when usually they were half-lidded from squinting against the glare of twenty-odd years spent riding the ranges in open country. McMullin was the oldest in the group and the most experienced. And in the man's eyes, Ren saw indecision, maybe even a little fear.

"The numbers are on our side," Ren repeated for the third time since starting the talk. "Even Ian Murphy isn't likely to tackle six-to-one odds. We only have to keep him away from the herd and order him off Logan's place."

"You sure it's him coming, Ren?" Jake Steele said.

"That's what Logan said. He said Murphy introduced himself."

"I dunno, Ren," Leo Hibbs said. "We're talkin' about Ian Murphy. I saw him in a fight up in Dodge one time. He's lightning-fast and no mere mortal. I doubt six-to-one is going to cut any ice with Ian Murphy."

Marion Franks spoke up. "Logan has already paid us. So I say we light a shuck and let him worry about Murphy. It's his trouble, not ours. It's pretty hard to spend money if you're dead."

Ren shook his head. "We have a profitable arrangement with Logan. You want to throw that away by running out on him? Besides, word would get out, and we'd have a devil of a time finding anyone else willing to deal with us. No one would trust us. So we have to see this through."

"So, what are we aiming to do?" Newell said.

"When Murphy shows, we'll brace him, and I'll tell him he's not cutting the herd. Then I'll tell him to get off the place."

"I don't like it," McMullin said finally. "Sure, if there's a fight, we might get the bulge on Murphy, but not without him killing some of us first."

"But you're assuming Murphy is willing to die over someone else's cows. Being a killer doesn't make him stupid. I don't think he'll push it. And once he leaves, I'll ride into town and talk to Tom Hale. Then Tom will take care of Murphy."

"I sure hope you're right about this, Ren," Franks said, his face tight and redder than usual. I ain't hankering to die over someone else's cows either."

"Just do as I say, and things will go fine. Spread out, and don't bunch up. I'll do the talkin' with Newell standing beside me with his scattergun. I'm telling you, boys, even Ian Murphy will not want to tackle the odds when he sees we mean business."

Jake Steele and Marion Franks got up and stretched and then stood around awkwardly, looking at the dead fire, their boots, and each other. Franks pulled a bandana from his pocket and mopped his face with it. Steele pushed his gun belt lower and looked at Ren. Ren could tell no one in the outfit was eager to go up against a man of Murphy's reputation. Then Burt McMullin got up. He walked over to his horse, pulled his Winchester from the boot, and dug inside a saddlebag for a box of cartridges.

Burt was the experienced hand, and the others respected him. They would stick now that Burt had shown he was going along with Ren's plan.

After loading the rifle, McMullin eased back onto the ground with his hands behind his head and his hat tilted over his face to wait. Everyone else went through the motions of acting natural, but fidgeted and acted restless while avoiding eye contact with Ren. The men looked a little too anxious to suit Ren. But maybe it was only restlessness. He supposed he'd know one way or the other when Murphy showed up.

# Chapter Five

## Cutting the Herd

Murphy and Maria rode side by side in silence for a distance, and then she turned her head and looked at him.

"What's going to happen, Señor Murphy?"

Murphy grinned. "Señor Murphy is such a mouthful. Why not just call me Ian?"

"As you wish, Ian."

Murphy nodded. "As to your question, I expect there to be men with the cattle who will try to discourage me from cutting the herd. I reckon Logan will have warned them by now."

"But you will insist on inspecting the brands?"

"I'll ask nicely first, but yep. I'll insist if it becomes necessary."

"So, there will be trouble."

"That all depends on them. I'm not hunting trouble."

"But you will use your gun if they refuse you?"

"If I must."

"The woman at the boarding house said you're a noted gunman. Are you a killer, Ian?"

"I've killed men, but only when they gave me no other choice."

"But if it is your habit to solve problems like this with a gun, can you claim to be blameless?"

"Señorita, a gun is a tool, no better or worse than a hammer, a shovel, or any other tool. A gun is as good or bad as the man using it and why he uses it. Unfortunately, there is little law west of the Pecos, the restraining influence men need here like everywhere else. A man has the right to protect his life and his property."

As much as she disliked the idea of consorting with a killer, Maria allowed that she might have rushed to judgment about this man Ian Murphy. He didn't seem a bad man, even though Logan's reaction to Murphy's name had shocked her. But, despite herself, Maria was more fascinated than repelled. More than that, she admitted she already felt a strange attraction to this soft-spoken and well-mannered man despite his reputation. Back home, men had courted her, but none had provided the spark she longed to feel for the man with whom she might choose to share her life. Yet, riding beside her, it seemed, was a man more than capable of producing such a spark. And she hardly knew him.

"What do you plan to do with the cattle, anyway?" Murphy said. "Stock a new range?"

"Señor Logan offered to sell me twelve-hundred steers and three hundred head of breeding stock," she said. "We need the steers to fulfill a contract my father made with the government to provide beef to feed the Indios on the reservations near our rancho. But I also intend to build our herd with the breeding stock so that the rancho can meet future contracts from its own herd instead of buying cattle."

"I see."

"But as badly as I need the cattle, I have no intention of buying stolen cattle. That's why I insisted that Señor Logan permit you to cut his herd."

"But if I'm right, and he has Flying X stock running with his herd, Logan won't be able to keep the agreement. I suspect most of the cattle he planned to sell you belong to the Flying X."

"Yes, that would cause my father and me great difficulty," Maria said. "I'm unsure where we might find other sufficient cattle to buy on such short notice. I had planned to drive the cattle from here directly to the army fort, where we've agreed to deliver the contracted cattle."

"It's only speculation until I've cut the herd, but if it turns out Logan has stolen Flying X beef on his spread, maybe you and I can strike a bargain, and you could still get your cattle."

"You would sell the cattle to me?"

"I have the authority. The man I represent owns a big spread over at Fort Stockton. He wants back what's his. But he'd be as happy with cash money as getting his cattle back. He'd have to send his hands here to drive them back to Fort Stockton."

"All right. If the cattle belong to this man, that would be acceptable, as long as you will meet Logan's price."

A few minutes later, Murphy and Maria saw the herd in the distance on the far side of a mesquite thicket. As they drew closer, Murphy counted six men getting to their feet who had been sheltering from the blistering sun beneath the thorny trees.

"The reception committee is forming," Murphy said.

"There are six men," Maria said. "I don't think you will cut the herd without their permission. It's too many."

"I'd rather face six any time than one determined, tough fighting man."

"What? Why? You're outnumbered six to one. Well, six to two, if you count me. Still, I must admire your idea of fair odds."

"When you have a group of men, someone has to take the lead," Murphy said. "Nobody wants that job because he can be sure if the shooting starts, he'll probably be the first one killed. And out of the six, you can bet no more than half have any stomach for a fight."

"I suppose we're about to find out," Maria said.

Murphy surveyed the group. Two men stood out front, awaiting their arrival. The other four stood spread out behind them. All wore gun belts. One man in front held a scattergun across his chest, telling Murphy something. Cow punchers didn't carry scatterguns, but a rustler might. One man in the group of four behind the two in front held a rifle.

Murphy and Maria rode up to the group and stopped about a dozen feet away.

"You Murphy?" one man said. He was a big, strongly built man with dark whisker stubble on his face, red from the sun.

"That's right."

The air was still, and heat waves rippled as the sun blazed down from the hot, copper sky.

"We work for Logan," the man said. "You're not cutting our herd, so why don't you and the lady just turn around now, ride back to town, and save yourselves a lot of trouble?"

"We don't want trouble, but I'm cutting the herd," Murphy said flatly. His eyes had turned dark and hard, and he felt something rising strong and hot inside him. He walked his horse nearer to the two men. "And I expect you've got Flying X stock running with it."

The man with the scattergun cocked both hammers.

"Turn around and ride on," the unshaven man said, but with less conviction in his tone than before. Murphy saw the indecision in his eyes.

"If you think I'm bluffing, suppose you grab that pistol," Murphy said.

Oppressive silence hung in the air. Baldwin Ren wanted to act, but he knew he was looking into the eyes of death. Suddenly, he knew all the brave talk he had spoken to his outfit less than half an hour before had been only that. Just talk.

Murphy stepped his horse closer. "Come on, damn you," he said. "If you want trouble, start it. Otherwise, step aside and let me do what I came to do."

Zeke Newell, the man with the scattergun, never really knew why he did it. Maybe it was his fighting pride and how the tall stranger talked down to his friend Ren like he was nothing. Nevertheless, he swung the scattergun around toward Murphy. Ren, seized by a moment of inspiration, grabbed at his gun butt. But both were too slow. The Colt that suddenly appeared in Murphy's hand spat flame. Two well-aimed shots. The first bullet clipped Newell's right upper arm, and he dropped the scattergun. The second drilled the web of Ren's right hand as he cleared leather and sent his pistol flying away. Then, as suddenly as it had appeared, Murphy's Colt was back in the holster.

Murphy eyed the four men behind Ren and Newell as he took a cigar out of his shirt pocket and put it between his lips. Then, producing a match from the other pocket, he struck it on his saddle horn and lit the cigar. His gray, flat eyes roved from man to man as he smoked. Ren wrapped his bandana around his wounded hand, and Newell stood with his left hand clapped over his bloodied right arm.

When the fight started, Maria had spurred her horse about ten yards away from Murphy and had drawn her silver-plated Colt, placing the men on foot in peril of a crossfire.

As Murphy's eyes seemed to bore a hole straight through him and seeing the woman's drawn pistol, Burt McMullin slowly and carefully laid his Winchester on the ground as the other three men near him kept their hands well away from their guns.

"Unless anyone else has objections, I'm cutting that herd," Murphy announced.

Two men reached to unbuckle their gun belts to make plain they had no objections.

"That's not necessary," Murphy said. "Keep your guns. You might feel lucky." Then he looked from Ren to Newell.

"I could have you killed you both. Agreed?"

Neither man replied.

"Well, you don't disagree. But I don't want to kill you. I told you, I didn't come here huntin' trouble. I'm only here looking for Flying X stock."

Sensing the crisis had passed, Maria holstered her Colt.

"You're playing a rough game, amigo," Ren said through clenched teeth, holding his wounded hand. "There's folks in this country who won't appreciate your manner."

"Nevertheless," Murphy said, swinging down from the saddle. "Any man who thinks of drawing chips in the game should first figure out what he can stand to lose."

Murphy strode over to McMullin and picked up the Winchester from the ground. Then, after levering the rifle until he'd ejected all the cartridges, he took the rifle by the barrel and flung it deep into the mesquite thicket.

"You trust us to keep our guns?" Jake Steele stammered with an incredulous look on his face.

A hint of a smile formed on Murphy's lips before he replied. "I'm sure you're all tough men, but none of you strike me as a damn fool." Then he returned to the roan and mounted.

Murphy looked at Maria and nodded. Then, as the six men watched, the unlikely pair skirted the group and rode toward the herd.

"I saw what you did back there," Murphy said. "Putting them in a crossfire. You're no tenderfoot, Señorita Espinosa."

The open admiration in Murphy's tone made Maria's heart swell with pride.

"In many ways, my father raised me as the son he never had," she said simply. Then, grinning broadly, she added, "And if I'm to call you Ian, you must call me Maria rather than Señorita Espinosa."

"As you wish, Maria," Murphy said with a wide smile.

Skirting the herd, Murphy grinned a little as they rode along. He immediately saw that someone had used a running iron to alter the Flying X brand into a Double Diamond.

"Might have even done that myself if I was a cattle thief," Murphy said. "Changing the Flying X to a Double Diamond is almost too simple to pass over." But then, more soberly, he added, "But I wouldn't have killed a man to do it. And I think that's what happened to Blair Ward and the four men with him."

"The rancher's son?"

Murphy nodded, seemingly deep in thought.

After riding through the herd for almost an hour, Murphy turned to Maria. "I estimate there is a full thousand head of Flying X stock here, maybe even more. But we'll have to cut them all out to get an accurate tally."

"I'll bring my vaqueros out in the morning, and we'll cut them out," Maria said. "If you intend to sell them to me."

"Sure do," Murphy said. "What price did Logan give you?"

"Eighteen dollars a head for the lot."

"Okay, well, there may not be twelve hundred Flying X steers here. And Colonel Ward said nothing about missing any breeding stock. So, I'll let you have the Flying X steers for fifteen a head to make up for your inconvenience. After that, it's up to you if you want to buy the breeding stock and the rest of the steers from Logan. But I'd be sort of inclined to be suspect of any Double Diamond-branded cows."

"I agree," Maria said. "After what we've seen, I'm no longer inclined to do business with Señor Logan. A thousand steers would be sufficient to meet the government contract. I can wait on the breeding stock if I must."

"Well, Colonel Ward has breeding stock back in Fort Stockton," Murphy said. "If you're interested, I'm sure he could supply all you want."

"Good," Maria said. "Given the circumstances, I'm in the market for a new supplier."

"Well, let's ride back to town," Murphy said. "Should be going on supper time when we get back to the boarding house, and we can make an early start in the morning."

"All right," Maria said, secretly happy that she and Murphy were lodging in the same boarding house. She hoped to spend more time with him before bedtime. "But I must stop at the camp of my vaqueros. I wish to alert my segundo about our plans for the morning."

"Sure thing. It's right on the way."

# Chapter Six

## The Gunslick

AFTER THE RUSTLERS WATCHED Murphy and the woman ride away towards the herd, Burt McMullin set about building a fire and setting water to boil. Then, as the man in the outfit most experienced with gunshot wounds, he took it on himself to see to Ren and Newell's wounds without anyone asking. Neither wound was serious, a good thing, since there was no doctor within sixty miles of Comanche Gap. Murphy's bullet had only burned Newell's upper right arm, barely breaking the skin but leaving an angry red welt behind. The second bullet had only notched the web of Ren's right hand instead of piercing straight through it.

"A half-inch further into the meat, and you might have lost the use of the thumb," McMullin said casually as he wrapped Ren's hand in a clean handkerchief from his saddlebag. "Both of you fellas are lucky Murphy didn't kill you."

"God almighty, he's fast," Jake Steele said. "I never saw anything like it."

"I warned you fellers," Leo Hibbs cackled. "I told you I saw him in a fight up in Dodge. The man is fast as a rattler's strike. Ian Murphy is not a man to fool about with."

Ren grimaced as McMullin drew the knot in the handkerchief tight over the wound to staunch the bleeding.

"If we had all acted together, we could have taken him," Ren growled, looking pointedly at McMullin.

"If we had all pulled iron on that hombre, we'd all be dead men," McMullin said. "That woman looked like she knew what she was about, too. She moved to the side to put us in a crossfire."

Newell sat cross-legged on the ground while McMullin cleaned the wound on his upper arm, saying nothing. It hadn't escaped him he had looked death squarely in the eye when he had foolishly tried to point the scattergun at Murphy. He felt lucky to be alive.

"So, what do we do now, Ren?" Marion Franks said. "I doubt that running iron trick will fool Murphy. He'll cut out the Flying X cows, and old Logan will demand his money back."

"He's not taking the cows from us," Ren said, standing up. "I'm riding into town to talk to Tom Hale. Tom will handle Murphy the same as that kid who came looking for the cattle."

"I doubt it," Leo Hibbs said, pulling out the makings and building a smoke. "Hale is fast, but he's no Ian Murphy. I doubt Hardin could beat Murphy."

"I wouldn't say that to Tom's face if I were you," Ren growled. "Why don't you make yourself useful for once, Hibbs, and saddled my bronc."

Hibbs cast Ren a wry grin, and then he headed off to saddle the man's horse.

When Hibbs led his horse over, Ren took the reins in his left hand, grabbed the saddle horn, and climbed aboard with a wince.

"I'll be back in a couple of hours," he said to the others. "Jake, it's your turn. Rustle up some grub before I get back."

"Okay, boss."

Ren spurred his horse and galloped toward town. After he was out of earshot, Steele turned to the others.

"I don't know about you fellers. It took me a long time to learn my elbow from a hot rock. But I've already had my fill of Ian Murphy after seeing him up close and personal. So I'm sure not tackling that man."

"I second the motion," Marion Franks said. "We got Logan's money. I say when Ren gets back, we ask for our shares and drift out of here until Murphy leaves the country."

"Ren will never quit," Newell said. "He'd take what you're sayin' as a double-cross, Franks. Ren would kill any man who asked for his share with the idea of quittin' this outfit and drifting away from here."

"But there won't be any money once Murphy takes those cows," Steele argued. "Logan will demand the money back that he paid us."

"And if we all throw in together on it, Ren can't take us all on," Franks said. "Not with his hand shot up. We did the work, and we all deserve our shares of that money."

"Let's wait till Ren gets back, and we hear what he says about Tom Hale," McMullin said, spitting a stream of tobacco juice on the ground. "If Hale takes Murphy off the board, that will solve the problem."

"If, brother," Hibbs said. "If he takes Murphy off the board. You all saw him in action. If anyone wants to take bets, I won't put my money on Hale against Ian Murphy.

Not unless Hale shoots the man in the back while he ain't lookin.'"

"Hibbs, you better watch your bucket mouth talkin' that way about Tom Hale," Newell said. "If he should hear about it, Ian Murphy will be the least of your problems."

Hibbs grinned anxiously. "Oh, Zeke, I was only foolin' about. I wasn't serious about suggestin' Tom Hale would back shoot a man. But I don't believe he is near as fast as Murphy. That's all I'm sayin.'"

BALDWIN REN WAS IN a foul mood when he arrived in Comanche Gap. His hand hurt something fierce, and he knew he'd dropped a peg or two in the eyes of the outfit after what had happened at the cow camp. He had to strike a deal with Tom Hale before Ian Murphy took back the Flying X stock. He reckoned the outfit would come apart if that happened, since none of them, besides Newell, had shown any stomach for the fight with Murphy. Ren tied his horse to the hitching rail outside the cantina and went inside.

Ren found Hale sitting at a table, playing cards with two cow punchers. They were two of the four men that had ridden into town with the Ward kid, but neither had been Flying X hands. Instead, they were just two layabouts Ward had hired to help him recover the cattle missing from Ward's ranch. The other two, both dead and buried, had been Flying X ranch hands. These two gents had accepted Ren's offer of twenty dollars each to kill their companions. Then Hale had done for the Ward whelp after pushing him into a fight. Since then, the two saddle bums had stayed in Comanche Gap, hanging around with Tom Hale.

"You boys having a good game?" Ren said as he walked up to the table.

"Well, Tom sure is," the cowboy named Slim Larson said, throwing his hand face down on the table in disgust. "I fold."

A shadow of a smile crossed Hale's face. "Guess it isn't your day, Larson."

"Nor mine," the other cowboy said, putting his cards face down on the table. "I fold, too."

Hale laughed and raked in the pot. He was a broad-shouldered man with a trim waist, brown eyes, and dark blond curly hair that fell to his shoulders. He wore his usual dress—a black flat-crowned hat, white broadcloth shirt beneath a black vest, and gray wool pants stuffed inside his black boots. But what people usually noticed first about Hale were the two tied-down Colts belted around his waist.

Rumor was that Hale had drifted to Texas and Comanche Gap after killing a lawman in Leadville, Colorado, to avoid arrest for murder. Otto Schmidt, the owner of the cantina and most everything else in Comanche Gap, had hired Hale as a poker dealer and to keep order in the saloon when crowds grew rowdy.

Hale looked up at Ren but said nothing. The question was on his hawkish face, and he didn't have to ask it. So Ren spoke up.

"Ian Murphy showed up at the cattle camp and played hob," he said, holding up his hand wrapped in the blood-stained handkerchief for emphasis.

"Sit and tell me about it," Hale said. Then he glanced at the two cowboys. "Give us some space."

The men nodded, got up, and sauntered over to the bar. Ren dragged out a chair and sat down. Hale picked up a cup and took a sip, peering at Ren over the lip. Ren had never seen the man drink whiskey, but he always seemed to have a cup of black coffee at hand. Ren related the story of what had happened at the camp when Ian Murphy and some Mex woman had shown up to cut the herd.

"Who is the woman?"

"I expect she's the woman Logan intends to sell the cows to, but she didn't introduce herself."

Hale nodded. "It's definite? The man was Ian Murphy?"

"Yeah, no doubt about it. Leo Hibbs recognized him—he saw Murphy up in Dodge once."

Hale nodded again and set his cup down. "Heard of him. He's fast and sure with a gun."

"He was too fast and sure for Newell and me," Ren said bitterly. "I can attest to that."

"How bad did Newell get it?"

"The bullet only burned his right upper arm—hardly broke the skin."

"I'd say you two boys are lucky you're still breathing after tackling a man like that."

"Yeah, it was foolish. But Murphy's manner riled up Newell, and when he swung his scattergun up, I thought I had an edge and palmed my pistol."

"And he shot you both."

"That's about the size of it."

"So, what do you want?"

"I want to hire you to kill Murphy. He'll probably be out to cut out those Flying X cows tomorrow morning. Then I'll have trouble with Logan."

"What does Logan have to say about it?"

"Nothing yet. He was out at the camp but had already left before Murphy showed up."

"So, who is paying me?"

"I will, and I've got the money in my saddlebags. Name the price."

"Well, Ian Murphy is no wet behind the ears pup," Hale said. "I can wipe him out for you, but the price is two hundred dollars."

"Two hundred?" Ren winced.

"That's what I said. Of course, you and your outfit can make another run at him if you're of a mind to save money."

"Uh, no," Ren stammered. "Two hundred sounds about right, Tom."

"Okay, then," Hale said, nodding. "Get the money. I'll take care of it as soon as I find he's back in town."

Ren nodded, got up, and walked outside. He returned two minutes later and handed Hale the two hundred dollars.

"He still at the camp when you left?" Walker said.

"Yeah, checking brands."

"Alright, I'll have Slim and Rex keep a lookout for him. Then, when he gets back here, I'll take care of it for you."

"Appreciate it," Ren said. "Guess I'll get back to the camp." Then he turned and left the saloon.

The two saddle bums glanced at Hale, who gestured them back over to his table. He told Rex Walker to find a place in the shadows near the livery. He told Slim to loaf around the boarding house and then told them whoever saw Murphy and the Mex woman first to bring him the word.

# Chapter Seven

## The Vaqueros

As THEY STARTED BACK toward town, riding side by side, Murphy caught himself casting sidelong glances at Maria. She was tall, elegant, her skin a beautiful olive, her eyes—

Maria caught him looking. She smiled a little, her eyes widened, and her lips parted slightly. Although the woman hadn't seemed to mind him looking, he had hurriedly looked away, his face flushed. Murphy liked women well enough, but he'd never tried to enter a relationship with one because of his past and reputation as a gunman. What could he offer a woman, any woman? He was a drifter, a man with a gun always walking along the thin line between life and death. And it took so little to fall. He might have a few weeks or months to live. Death could come tomorrow. But here was a woman he could imagine spending his life with, although he knew there was no chance of it happening.

"You think those men will cause trouble tomorrow?" Maria said.

Murphy looked at her. He watched her lips, the rise of her breasts as she spoke, the wetness of her lips. He turned away quickly, feeling a sharp pain in his chest.

"It doesn't matter," he said finally. "We're taking those Flying X cattle back, one way or another. But if there's trouble, I think Logan will have to find others for the job. I reckon we cured those boys back there of hunting trouble with us."

"I hope you're right about them, Ian. And I hope Señor Logan makes no further trouble. Perhaps after he speaks with those men, he will understand he must relinquish title to the stolen cattle."

"I guess we'll find out soon enough."

The pair rode into the camp of Maria's vaqueros near the spring above the gap as the men prepared supper over an open fire.

A big man, broad-shouldered and powerful, stepped forward. He had a handsome yet savage face. The man wore a black sombrero, a black neckerchief, and a dark gray jacket with a cut-away front and silver buttons over a gray shirt. He had his gray wool pants stuffed into tall leather boots adorned with the large-roweled silver spurs favored by vaqueros. Around his waist, the man had tied a red sash, and over it wore a black leather gun belt with a pearl-handled silver-plated Colt. The man removed his sombrero as he approached and spoke in Spanish to Maria in measured tones. She replied in Spanish.

Murphy knew a little Spanish but wasn't fluent in the language and didn't understand the entire exchange. But he could tell two things. First, the man referred to Maria as *jefe*, which meant boss. Second, the man had asked her several questions about him. Finally, after a few minutes, Maria turned to Murphy. "This is Antonio, my *segundo*."

Murphy nodded to Antonio, and the man nodded in return, but said nothing. Antonio gazed at him, but Murphy detected no hostility. Perhaps he had Maria to thank for that.

"I've explained to Antonio about the stolen cattle and the change of our plans," Maria said. "He will have the men ready to ride at dawn."

Murphy nodded. "Okay."

Maria said a few more words to Antonio. He replied, then turned and walked toward the fire, putting his sombrero back on his head.

"Now we can return to our lodging place and have supper," she said to Murphy.

"Suits me," Murphy said, turning his horse toward the town. Maria followed.

⁓⁓

REX WALKER HAD FOLLOWED Tom Hale's instructions and had found a shadowed corner from which he could watch the comings and goings at the livery. After half an hour, he had seen neither hide nor hair of the man Murphy or the Mexican woman. But he saw something else, in particular someone else, that interested him, though. He saw old Charlie Henry leading his burro out of the livery, loaded with supplies that Walker reckoned the old man had picked up from the mercantile. Charlie Henry, or more to the point, the rumor Rex and his saddle mate Slim had heard about Henry, was why they had stayed on at Comanche Gap. The rumor the men had heard from someone in the cantina was that Henry was prospecting for gold and silver in the nearby hills.

But, of course, he was not prospecting in the ordinary sense. As far as Rex and Slim, or anyone else, knew, there was no gold or silver ore to be found anywhere around the Pecos' country. There had never been. But most everyone in that part of Texas had heard the stories about Emperor Maximilian's treasure.

Once the Mexican emperor realized his countrymen intended to depose him back in 1866, he tried to sneak his wealth out of the country before fleeing to Europe. Since the rebels controlled all the ports, Maximilian chose four Austrian officers and some Mexican royalists to transport his wealth north to Port Galveston in Texas for shipping back to Europe.

Maximilian's loyalists loaded millions in gold bars, silver, jewelry, and other valuables into oxen-drawn wagons and transported the treasure north. Eventually, the men arrived safely in Texas with their cargo intact. Once they were over the Rio Grande, they camped shortly at the Presidio del Norte. There, they met six former Confederate soldiers heading to Mexico.

Texas had been dangerous with all the Comanche raids and banditry back then. So, to help safeguard the cargo, the Austrian officers hired the six men to guide them to the Galveston. At first, the former confederates didn't know what was in the cargo and agreed to escort the transport. But somewhere near Comanche Gap, the men learned what was in the wagon. They killed the Austrians and their Mexican loyalists and took the wealth for themselves. But they soon learned they could not take all the loot by themselves. So, taking only a little of the gold, they buried the rest of the treasure somewhere near the gap, intending to reorganize and return for it later.

Shortly after leaving the treasure behind, one bandit fell ill, and the others left him behind. After a few days' rest, the man got better and hurried to catch up with the others. But after traveling only a short distance from where he had rested, he came upon the rotting bodies of his comrades. Comanches had killed them all.

The lone survivor traveled alone back north but, again falling ill, had to stop at a small town in north Texas to see a doctor. His illness worsened, and according to the story, knowing he would not recover, the man told the doctor who had treated him well about the treasure. He even drew a rudimentary map of where they had buried the treasure. Once the last bandit died, the doctor organized a party that traveled to Comanche Gap seeking the treasure. But after weeks of searching in vain, they gave up.

The man at the cantina had told Rex and Slim that Charlie Henry had come into possession of the map. Then he had come to Comanche Gap to look for the treasure. The man also said that Charlie had used some old Mexican gold and silver coins to purchase supplies at the mercantile, which proved Charlie had already found some of the treasure. But, though many had tried, no one had successfully tracked Charlie back to his diggings from town. So Rex and Slim decided that the next time they saw Henry in town, they would just force him to tell them where the treasure was. And here was Rex's chance. He forgot all about Murphy and the woman, sauntered across the street, and blocked Charlie Henry's path.

# Chapter Eight

## Murphy Uses His Fists

As Murphy and Maria walked their horses toward the livery, Murphy saw a sight that made him coldly and bitterly furious. An older man lay on the ground in front of the livery. Curled into a ball, he had his hands up, covering his face. A bigger, younger man standing over him was putting his boots to the man on the ground, cursing and shouting down at him. Murphy spurred the roan into a gallop, and when he got to the men, he jerked the horse to a stop and leaped from the saddle. The attitude of the younger man, his bullying voice, and his vicious attack on the downed man enraged Murphy. Suddenly aware of Murphy, the younger man whirled toward him just as Murphy's right fist exploded toward him. The punch was so swift and unexpected that the big man could not avoid it, and Murphy's fist smashed under his jaw. The blow slammed his head back on his neck, and the man tottered. Murphy stepped in and struck him with his left fist. That punch opened a cut on the man's upper lip and bloodied his nose. The man went to his knees. Then Murphy delivered another devastating right that sent the man face down on the dirt street.

Loitering near the boarding house, Slim watched the one-sided fight in disbelief and then broke into a dead run toward the livery to help his friend Rex. But Murphy heard him coming and turned to meet him. When he stepped in to meet Slim, he struck swiftly. After whipping an underhand punch to Slim's wind, Murphy followed with a left hook to Slim's face and then put Slim out of the running with a straight right that connected with Slim's chin. Slim's knees caved. He pitched forward, face-first into the dirt.

Murphy walked to the older man on the ground, took him by the arm, and helped him to his feet.

"You alright, old-timer?" Murphy said.

"I've been better," the man groaned, obviously shaken by the ordeal and holding a hand to his ribs on the right side.

"Never could tolerate someone putting the boots to man after he was down," Murphy said.

"Much obliged, stranger," the older man said. "I thought the big feller would stomp the life out of me."

"What was it all about, anyway?"

"Those two polecats have been laying for me," the man said. "I've done my best to avoid them, but that big feller caught me unawares coming out of the livery."

"Who are they?"

"Just a couple of saddle bums, layabouts from over Fort Stockton way. They intended to rob me."

"Well, it doesn't look like they will bother you further today," Murphy said, looking at the two unconscious cowboys lying in the dirt.

"Yeah, I better catch Bessie and head to my camp before they come to," the man said, backing away. The suddenness and violence of his rescuer frightened him almost as much as Rex had. He grabbed the rope tied to the burros' halter and shuffled away, leading the animal, and still holding his ribs.

Murphy noticed the man seemed strangely attired for the Pecos country as he watched the man depart. He wore clothes like those of the miners Murphy had seen when passing through Leadville, Colorado. But Murphy knew there were no gold or silver mines anywhere in West Texas. Then he turned to notice Maria standing behind him, holding the reins of both horses.

Maria Espinosa stared dumbfounded at the two men lying in the dirt. It had astonished her that Murphy had beaten them both unconscious in the space of only a few moments. Murphy's quick temper and capacity for violence frightened her, yet strangely excited her at the same time. And had his actions not been just? She had witnessed the one man abusing the helpless, elderly gringo when she and Murphy had ridden up. And it had seemed the other had intended to attack Murphy.

A heavy set man carrying a pitchfork and a young boy, the stable hand Murphy had dealt with before, rounded the corner of the livery at a run. They both skidded to a stop, gaping at the two cowboys lying unconscious in front of the stable.

"I'm Carl Abernathy, the owner of this here livery," said the man to Murphy. "I was out back forkin' hay to the stock in the corral when the boy came runnin' to tell me someone was beating old Charlie Henry. But it seems like you've taken things well in hand."

"Yeah, the big fella there was puttin' his boots to the old timer when we rode up," Murphy said. "You know these two coyotes?"

"Only by their names," Abernathy said. "That there is Rex Walker and Slim Larson. They are a couple of no accounts, if I've ever seen any. They rode into town with a young rancher fella and two other gents a while back."

"A young rancher riding a buckskin gelding with a Flying X brand?"

"Yes, sir, he surely was. A young fella name of Ward, I recollect."

"You know what happened to Ward and the two other cowboys?" Murphy asked.

"Well, I can't say what happened to the other two, but that young fella let Tom Hale bait him into a fight over at the cantina. He grabbed iron and got hisself killed."

"Were the two others present when it happened?"

"No, sir," Abernathy said. "Day after they rode in, those fellas rode out of town with these two. And they never came back. I can't say for sure, mind you, but judging by the character of these two boys, it wouldn't surprise me none to learn those gents occupy lonely graves out there in the desert somewhere."

"Appreciate the information," Murphy said. "And I expect you're right about things."

"I'll take your horses, mister," the boy said.

Murphy nodded, and taking the reins from Espinosa, handed them over to the stable boy. "Thanks, Jimmy. Appreciate it."

The boy led the animals into the livery stable while Abernathy studied the men on the ground, who were still unconscious.

"We've got no doctor hereabouts," he said finally. "Not sure what to do with them, although I suppose we can't leave them here in the street."

"I'll ask a favor, if you don't mind," Murphy said.

"What is it?"

"I'd like to drag these two into your stable and tie them up for a spell. Then I'd like to ask them a question or two when they come around. But I'd need you to keep a watch on them, and I'm willing to pay you."

Abernathy scratched his chin. "You the law or something, mister?"

"I'm justice, but not the law," Murphy said evenly.

Abernathy's eyes widened. "Justice?"

"Or vengeance, if you prefer," Murphy said. "I aim to make those responsible pay for what they did to Blair Ward and those two ranch hands."

Abernathy nodded solemnly. "Then I guess I'll accommodate you. But I'd appreciate it if you didn't drag things out too long. There are those in this town who might hold it against me for helping you."

"I only need a few hours until they come around and can talk," Murphy said. "Then, one way or another, I'll take them off your hands."

"All right, mister. Give me a hand and we'll drag them inside. I've got plenty of good rope in there."

# Chapter Nine

## Provoked to Violence

AFTER TAKING THEIR GUNS and tying up the two drifters, Murphy left them in Abernathy's charge. Then he and Maria walked together to the boarding house. Espinosa had many questions she wanted to ask, but said nothing until they sat down at a table in the dining room. Harry Fisher set two plates on the table before them and, after shooting Espinosa an angry look, she withdrew to the kitchen.

"Will you kill those men, Ian?" Espinosa blurted, unable to restrain herself any longer.

"I'm considering it," he said, after swallowing a mouthful of food.

"But you are not a lawman."

"There is no law in Comanche Gap," Murphy said. "Sometimes a man must dispense justice the best way he can."

"But you heard the stableman," Espinosa argued. "He said he was unsure whether those men killed the others."

"That's why I mean to give them a chance to talk first," Murphy said.

"And if they refuse to answer your questions? Then what? You will kill them? Just like that?"

"Maybe so."

Espinosa shook her head angrily. "I had convinced myself you were not a killer," she said, "though you are a gunman. Now, I am not so sure."

"Those men likely killed two of the men from my ranch," Murphy said. "What should I do? Turn the other cheek and forget it?"

"No, not if they are guilty. But you have laws in Texas, do you not? Do they not deserve a trial before you punish them?"

"It's sixty miles to the nearest law and jail." Murphy said, irritation creeping into his tone. "I have no time for that. I've got more important things to attend to here."

"So, you intend to kill them, as a matter of convenience. I see."

"Can we talk about something else?" Murphy said.

"No," Maria said, feeling frustrated. She stood up without touching her food. "I had wished to speak to you more this evening. So that we might become better acquainted. But no more. I'm retiring to my room." With that, Espinosa turned angrily on her heel and strode from the room.

Murphy shook his head. Women, he thought. Who could understand them? At least now he could finish his meal in peace.

After finishing his supper, Murphy left the boarding house and walked back to the livery. Darkness had fallen and the night air felt somewhat cooler. He found Carl Abernathy sitting on an overturned bucket outside the stable doors. The man stood as Murphy approached.

"I'm glad you're back," Abernathy said. "They came around a little while after you left with the lady. And they're powerful mad at us for tying them up."

"Don't worry," Murphy said. "I'll ask my questions and get them out of here. I promise none of it will come back to you."

"I'm not so sure," Abernathy said. "They allowed they knew I was in on it with you. They might be no account saddle bums, but that don't mean they won't come for me once you turn them loose."

"Who said anything about turning them loose?" Murphy said. "I only said I'd have them out of your livery soon."

Abernathy's eyes widened. "You mean—"

"The less you know, the better," Murphy said. "Why don't you head home? I'll take it from here."

Abernathy nodded woodenly and walked away into the darkness. Murphy opened the door and walked inside. He found Walker and Larson in the stall where he'd left them with their wrists and ankles tied.

"You're a dead man," Larson spat when he saw Murphy enter the stall. "When Hale finds out what you've done, he will kill you."

"You two made a big mistake," Murphy said.

"What are you talking about?" Walker sputtered.

"It's never a good idea to provoke a man to violence who has spent his whole life perfecting it," Murphy said. "But that's what you did when you killed those two cowboys. They were my friends."

"We killed no one," Larson said. "You're wrong. Now turn us loose, damn you."

"Not until you've answered a question or two," Murphy said.

"You're crazy," Walker said. "You're not the law, you're nothin'. We ain't telling you squat."

"Well, that's up to you," Murphy said coldly. "No, I'm not the law. But I ain't nothin'. For you two, I'm the judge and jury and the executioner. I'm justice."

Walker and Larson stared at Murphy, suddenly at a loss for words.

Murphy sat on the overturned bucket he'd carried inside with him. "I'll start with you," he said, pointing at Walker. "Where did you bury Conway and Davis? Or did you just leave them out in the desert to rot after you killed them?"

"I've got nothin' to say to you," Walker said.

Murphy bent over and picked up a coiled rope he'd taken from a hook inside the livery.

"Better reconsider your position," Murphy said. Deftly, he began fashioning a noose at one end of the rope.

"What do aim to do with that?" Larson cried.

"Gents, murder is a hanging offense in Texas, last I heard."

"But we told you, we killed no one," Larson whined.

"I beg to differ," Murphy said, finishing the thirteenth and final wrap before knotting the noose.

"You're bluffing," Walker said, but without confidence.

"Am I?" Murphy said with a wry grin.

Standing, Murphy carried the bucket out of the stall and centered it beneath a large beam above the ground. Then he threw the noose end of the rope over the beam and standing atop the bucket, positioned it at the proper height. Stepping off the bucket, he made the other end of the rope fast to a post in a corner of the stall. Then, he stooped and grabbed Walker by an arm and dragged him out of the stall. After hoisting the man to his feet,

Murphy bodily picked him up and stood him atop the overturned bucket.

"You stand there," Murphy growled. "You jump off that bucket and I'll just put you back up there after knocking your front teeth out."

Murphy walked away from Walker and then returned with a wooden crate. He set it beside the bucket, stood on it, and looped the noose over Walker's head. After positioning the knot behind Walker's right ear, Murphy cinched it tight. Then he stepped down from the crate.

"You don't have to do this," Walker cried.

"They always say that," Walker said, shaking his head. "Say what?"

"Every bad man I ever met always says, you don't have to do this when justice comes calling for them."

"We had no choice," Walker cried in panic. "A fella over at the cantina made us kill those boys. We had no choice. It was them or us. That's what the man said."

"So you killed my friends," Murphy said. "That's what you're saying?"

"Yes, but it wasn't our idea. We had no choice."

"Who made you kill them?" Murphy asked, feigning sympathy.

"I can't tell you that. He'd kill us. He warned us to keep our mouths shut."

"Considering you're standing on top of a bucket with a noose around your neck, I think you must."

"All right, damn you. A fella name of Ren, Baldwin Ren. He works on a ranch outside of town."

"The Double Diamond?"

"That sounds right."

"So, how did you get them out of town to kill them?"

"Well, after Ward turned in for the night over at the boarding house, we went to the room Conway and Davis were in. Slim told them a fella at the cantina told us where Ward's cows were, but that rustlers were about to move them. We convinced them to ride out there with us, without bothering Ward until we knew what was what."

"Then outside town, you shot them in the back?"

"I didn't want to do that way. But Slim said that was best, and I went along."

"You bury them, or leave them to the animals?"

"Of course, we buried them. Gave them a Christian burial. We aren't outlaws."

"So, you read from the book over them? You said a prayer?"

"Well, no, but we wrapped them in their rain slickers and buried them real deep. So the animals couldn't get to them."

"That was mighty Christian of you, brother," Murphy said sarcastically.

"We didn't want to do it, but we got scared after that Ren fella talked to us. We knew he meant business. I swear, it was them or us. And then Ren would have killed them, anyway."

"You two were so scared that afterwards, you've hung around here in Comanche Gap ever since?"

Walker flushed more deeply than he already was, but said nothing immediately. But then he cried, "You can't just hang us. We got a right to a trial. Take us to the law."

"Haven't you heard?" Murphy said coldly. "There is no law in Comanche Gap. The law don't go around here."

"You can't hang us without a trial."

"I've hanged my share of horse thieves when there was no law around. I guess I can hang a couple of murderers."

"Please, don't do this. I'm begging you, mister. It wasn't our doing."

"Go tell it to the devil," Murphy said coldly, and then he kicked the bucket from beneath Walker's bound feet.

Murphy had set the knot perfectly, and it snapped Walker's neck when he hit the end of the rope. After lowering the body and dragging it out of the way, Murphy tied the end of the rope back to the post after resetting the noose. Larson cried as Murphy dragged him out of the stall and stood him atop the bucket. Then, as Murphy adjusted the hangman's noose, Larson stopped crying and started cursing Murphy. Since he'd got all the answers he wanted from Walker, as soon as he stepped off the crate, he kicked the bucket from beneath Larson. Larson wasn't as lucky as Walker and kicked for several minutes before he died. Murphy regretted not taking more time to set the knot properly.

After lowering Larson's corpse, he got two horses from the corral and led them inside the livery. He hoisted Walker's body, belly down onto the back of a horse, and put Larson's body on the other. Then he led the horses out the back of the stable and down an alley to the back of the cantina. There, he untied the men's wrists and ankles before dragging their bodies off the horses. Leaving the corpses on the ground behind the cantina, he returned the horses to the livery stable's corral.

# Chapter Ten
## Cantina Show Down

FROM THE DOOR OF the livery stable, Murphy studied the street, still thinking about Conway and Davis. It was dark and quiet, and he saw no one moving about. Hanging Walker and Larson had given him no particular pleasure. Killing men never did. And he only killed when it had to be done. They had done for Conway and Davis and Murphy had done for them. He felt no remorse, and why should he? Neither had expressed remorse for murdering his two friends. They had offered only excuses. Weary now, all Murphy wanted was to return to the boarding house to get some shut eye. Every muscle felt fatigued. But he had one more thing to do first. Closing the door to the livery, he retraced his steps to the cantina, but this time to the front of the adobe. After loosening the Colt in the holster, he pushed through the front doors.

Pausing inside the doors, Murphy glanced around the room, allowing his eyes to adjust to the brightly lighted interior after walking in from the darkness outside. There at a table in a corner, he spotted Tom Hale dealing a hand of cards. Murphy strode to the bar, this time crowded. But Murphy found a spot to squeeze in and caught the eye of Walt Hansen, the surly bartender.

Hansen sauntered over and Murphy ordered a whiskey. After pouring the drink, Hansen moved leisurely down the bar to see to other customers. Murphy turned and leaned against the bar rail, the heel of his right boot resting on the brass foot rail running along the base of the bar and his right elbow resting on the bar. Holding the glass in his left hand, he sipped the rotgut whiskey, his eyes locked on Hale.

Predictably, Hale looked up after a time and met his gaze. Even across the distance between them, Murphy noted the look of surprise in Hale's eyes. It seemed Hale hadn't expected Murphy to appear, at least not now. It also seemed Hale found him a distraction, as his eyes flickered to Murphy frequently, instead of concentrating on his cards. Hale also glanced around the room as if looking for someone he expected to be there. Finally, Hale folded his hand, spoke to the men at his table, and got up. The pair of Colts belted low around Hale's waist didn't impress Murphy. A man who knew how to use a gun needed only one. Hale walked deliberately toward him.

Hale stopped close enough to converse with Murphy over the noise of the cantina crowd, but not too close.

"You must be Ian Murphy," said Hale contemptuously. "Heard of you."

"And I've heard of you, Hale," Murphy said flatly, fixing Hale with his implacable gray eyes.

"Nothing bad, I hope," Hale said with an insolent grin.

"I've heard you're a lowdown, yellow killer," Murphy said.

Hale's face seemed to tighten, and he hesitated, not liking it. He studied Murphy, puzzled. Murphy was so obviously in complete possession of himself, Hale found it unnerving.

"I ran into a couple of your boys," Murphy said. "Walker and Larson. That who you were looking for around the place?"

"What about them?" Hale said, his face suddenly deathly pale. "Where are the boys?"

"Lyin' out back of this adobe," Murphy said. "They're both pretty dead."

Hale swallowed hard.

"The jury came back with guilty verdicts, the judge pronounced the sentences, and the executioner carried them out."

"What are you talking about, Murphy?"

"I hanged them both until they were dead for murder."

"Just what exactly are you looking for, Murphy?" Hale said, looking incredulous.

"Justice, Hale, and I'm huntin' you," Murphy said brutally.

Hales eyes narrowed. He stared at Murphy warily, but disbelieving. Murphy made no move to grab his gun. He reclined leisurely with his right elbow on the bar. He just waited.

"I have no fight with you, Murphy," Hale said, his mouth suddenly dry, and for the first time in his life feeling a knot of fear growing inside him.

"You murdered Blair Ward, Hale. I'm here to settle up accounts."

"That was a straight up fight, Murphy," Hale said. "Blair pulled iron on me."

"Yeah, I heard you baited him into a fight. Sounds about right. I've also heard gunning drunk cowhands and back shooting lawmen is your meat. Now is your chance to face a full grown man and make a real reputation for yourself."

"The folks in here, they know he drew on me," Hale insisted. "I defended myself. You try anything now, and they'll all come down on you."

The cantina crowd had gone quiet, and every eye was on Hale and Murphy. The men standing to Murphy's right and left had melted away to get out of the line of fire. Here was Tom Hale, a man known as a dangerous gunman, and this gray-eyed stranger was talking to him like he was nothing. No one in the crowd yet knew Ian Murphy was in town and that they were looking at the legendary gunslinger from the cattle trail towns.

"Jerk those pistols, and get to work," Murphy cried, a cold rage settling over him. "You want folks around here to see you're yellow?"

He had pushed off the bar and now stood straight with his right hand hovering near the butt of his Colt. Hale stood with his hands well away from his guns, his hands now visibly shaking.

"You're wrong, Murphy," Hale said.

"You're a coward, Hale, and I have no use for cowards."

Hale jumped as if someone had slapped him. He glanced around the room wildly, noticing everyone was gaping at him and realizing no one intended to help him.

"Who paid you to kill Blair Ward, Hale? I don't calculate you had any reason to do it unless you got paid for it."

"Nobody." Hale continued, but Murphy's flat, dead-eyed stare stopped him.

"Look, I—"

Murphy cut him off. "You've got one minute," he said, pointing his Colt, which had seemed to leap into his hand. "Then you get a notch in your ear, and I reckon I won't miss."

Hale swallowed. "All right. It was Logan, Frank Logan."

Murphy holstered the Colt. Then he quickly stepped in close to Hale and backhanded him across the face.

"You ready to jerk those pistols now?"

Hale moved his hands further away from his holstered pistols.

"I didn't think so," Murphy said coldly. Then he reached and snatched both Colts from Hale's holsters, turned and pitched them onto the bar with a clatter. Turning back, he faced Hale again.

"Don't just stand there and bleed," he said. "You're through here, Hale. You haven't got the grit to do the job Otto Schmidt hired you to do. Get out. I'll give you the chance to ride."

Hale stood rooted to the floor, unable to move. Murphy side-stepped, grabbing Hale's collar in his left hand, and the back of the man's gun belt in his right, and ran him towards the doors. There he threw Hale through the bat-wings like a man might throw a sack of grain. Hale plowed face first into the dirt. Humiliated, he struggled to his feet.

"Now run, you cur," Murphy cried. "Coward or not, the day you see my face again will be your last."

Hale shuffled quickly away toward the livery, never looking back.

Murphy turned and strode back inside and up to the bar. The men parted, giving him plenty of room. He picked up his glass from the bar and downed the rest of the whiskey.

"What am I supposed to do with these?" Hansen the bartender asked, gesturing towards Hale's pistols still laying on the bar.

"Give them to him if he comes back," Murphy said. "Hale better arm himself because if I ever see him again, I'll kill him, even if he's too yellow to draw."

Murphy then turned and walked out of the Cantina.

# Chapter Eleven
## Business Proposition

ENRAGED BY THE HUMILIATION Ian Murphy had heaped upon him in front of the townsfolk back at the cantina, Tom Hale strode quickly to the livery stable. There he let himself in through the unlocked door and saddled his sorrel. Hale also found two six guns inside the stable he recognized as those that had belonged to Larson and Walker. After checking the loads, he shoved the pistols into his empty holsters. They weren't the nickel plated Colts with ivory handles Murphy had taken from him, but he at least had guns again. Hale then led his saddled horse out of the stable and mounted. He had to get out to the Double Diamond and the Baldwin Ren gang before they heard how he had backed down from Murphy. He needed their help if he was to strike back at Murphy and gain his revenge. Hale spurred the sorrel and rode at a gallop out of town toward Logan's ranch.

---

IAN MURPHY STRODE ANGRILY along the boardwalk the short distance from the cantina to the boarding house. He was angry that Tom Hale had proven himself a coward and had refused to fight. That had prevented him from avenging the murder of Blair Ward. Even in the West, you couldn't shoot a man down like a rabid dog who refused to fight in front of a crowd of witnesses. Not even in a two-bit, lawless town like Comanche Gap.

The code of the West allowed a man to kill another over any dispute as long as there was the appearance it was a fair fight, however slight it might be. That made it legal. But most Western men viewed killing a man, even an armed man, who refused to be drawn into a gun battle as murder. So Murphy had done all he could about Hale. He had exposed him as a coward in public and had stripped the man of every shred of dignity.

While Western men would not countenance murder, neither did they look upon cowardice with favor. The story about Hale shrinking from a gunfight would sweep the country like a range fire and Hale could not show his face in public anywhere the story became known. Others would scorn him and his demonstrated lack of courage when facing an equally skilled gunman. Murphy could only hope that Hale would come against him seeking revenge at a later time, giving him another opportunity to wreak vengeance.

The interior boarding house was dark when Murphy entered. Everyone, including the proprietress, Harry Fisher, had long since gone to bed, so the bath Murphy had requested earlier was unavailable. He went directly to his room. There he had removed his gun belt and was taking off his shirt when there was a tentative knock at the door. Pulling his shirt back on, Murphy slid the Colt from its holster and tiptoed to the door. Unlocking the door, he cracked it and looked out. To his surprise, he saw old Charlie Henry standing in the hallway.

"I thought you left town for your camp, old timer," Murphy said.

"I came back after it got dark," Henry said. "I'd like a word with you."

Murphy nodded, opened the door, and gestured Henry inside. Appearing nervous as a cat near a rocking chair, Henry came in and sat down on a rickety chair in the corner. Murphy put away the Colt and sat down on the edge of the bed.

"How's the ribs?" Murphy said.

The old prospector grinned, touching his side. "A little sore, but I've suffered worse."

Murphy nodded. "What did you want?"

"To offer you a business proposition," Henry said, a twinkle in his eyes.

"What kind of proposition?"

"I need a partner to help me carry gold and silver from my diggings to the bank in Odessa."

Thinking the old man senile, Murphy doubted his claim about having gold and silver, but spoke kindly to him.

"I've always understood there are no gold or silver mines anywhere in this country, old timer."

"That's right, young fella. I'm not jawing about ore. I'm talking about coins of gold and silver and gold bars. You ever hear tell of that old Mexican Emperor Maximilian?"

Murphy nodded. "The revolutionaries executed him after they drove the French out of Mexico."

"That's right, but not before he sent twelve wagon loads of gold and silver coins and other treasure north to Texas disguised as barrels of flour."

"Yes, I've heard the legends about Maximilian's treasure being buried somewhere around Presidio."

"What if I told you those stories weren't no legend?" Henry said, digging into a pocket. Then he flipped a gold coin to Murphy. "And they didn't bury the treasure at Presidio, but right here in these mountains around Comanche Gap."

Murphy examined the coin and found it was a twenty-peso gold piece struck in 1866, bearing the likeness of Archduke Maximilian.

"I met this doc up in north Texas that told me the story," the old prospector said. "He came into possession of a map and he and some men came here looking for the treasure years ago. But they found nothing. So, I bought the map from him and moseyed down here."

"You're saying you found it?"

"Only a small part of it," Henry cackled. "Once I got here, I was sure that doc and his partners got one landmark wrong. So, I tested my idea and, sure enough, I uncovered a cache of the old oak barrels stenciled with *La Harina* on the sides."

"Flour?"

"You bet, but inside some barrels, I found sacks of gold coins like that one there. Others had sacks of silver coins, and others bars of gold. I've only scratched the surface, but I have a good amount of the stuff uncovered laying about my camp already."

"And you want to transport it to a bank."

Henry nodded. "I had to use some of those coins for trade at the mercantile to buy supplies. Soon, rumors were thick as flies around the town about what I was up to. And then the layabouts around Comanche Gap tried to track me back to my diggings whenever I came to town for supplies. I'm afeared it's only a matter of time until they find the camp and rob me."

"Why come to me? You know nothing about me, old timer. Maybe I'll rob you myself."

Henry cackled again. "I don't think so. You came to my aid when Rex Walker had me down and was kickin' the stuffin' out of me. I figure only an honorable hombre would come to the aid of an old man he didn't even know. I think you're a man to ride the river with, young fella. That's why I want to hire you."

"To help you carry that gold and silver to Odessa."

"Yep, and I'll pay you five thousand in gold for your trouble."

For years, Murphy had dreamed of settling down somewhere, of buying a small spread and running his own cattle. But on a cowpuncher's monthly pay of forty and found it was near impossible to save enough money to stake a dream like that. With five thousand in gold, the dream would become attainable. It was more than enough to buy a modest ranch and stock its range with a small herd of cattle.

"I'm interested in your proposition," Murphy admitted. "But I came to Comanche Gap for a purpose and I've yet more to accomplish. I couldn't start right away. I can't drop what I'm doing here to see you safely to Odessa."

"I figured as much," Henry said. "I want to get away as soon as possible. But I bought enough grub and supplies to see me through the rest of the month. So, I can stay out at the diggings and keep my head down with no need to return to town. That would give you a couple of weeks to wrap up your other affairs."

Murphy scratched his chin. "Yes," he agreed. "I should accomplish what I came here for within that amount of time."

Henry cackled and slapped his thigh. "So we got us a deal, young fella?"

"We do," Murphy said, "as long as I don't get myself killed in the meantime."

Henry nodded and stood up. He passed Murphy a crude hand-drawn map with directions scribbled on it.

"That's where you can find me when you're ready," he said. "Memorize that and then burn it. I'd hate that paper to find its way into the hands of others."

"Understood," Murphy said, getting up. He walked to the door and let Henry out.

After bolting the door, after undressing, he wearily climbed into bed. Old Charlie Henry had certainly raised the ante, and Murphy felt even more impatient to finish what he'd come to Comanche Gap to do.

# Chapter Twelve

## The Outlaw Camp

BALDWIN REN LOOKED AT Tom Hale, the doubtful expression on his face clear in the firelight, and Hale didn't like it.

"I tell you, that's what happened," Hale cried. "He came up behind me in the cantina and shoved his gun in my back. Then he disarmed me and said he'd kill me if I didn't get out of town."

"And no one in the cantina lifted a finger?" Ren said. "That don't sound right."

"Would you pull on iron on Murphy when his Colt was already out of the leather?"

Ren thought it over. "Well, I guess not. But there must have been a lot of men there at the time, and all of them armed."

"They were afraid he'd gun me down if they made a move," Hale insisted. "And you know most of those boys in town have no stomach for a gunfight."

"You said you'd take care of him soon as he got back to town," Ren said. "I paid you two hundred dollars. Why didn't you?"

"He jumped me, I tell you. I never had the chance. I had Rex and Slim watching for him and the Mex woman to ride in. But somehow Murphy got the jump on them and killed them both. Then he jumped me at the cantina."

"Well, I see you got guns now. Ride back there and take care of business. If you're telling me the gospel and Murphy is afraid of taking you on in a straight up fight, it shouldn't be too hard. You're claimin' the man is a lowdown, dirty coward."

"Even a coward can be dangerous when his back is against the wall," Hale said. "We need to all go in together and take care of Murphy once and for all."

"Then what am I payin' you for, Tom?"

Angrily, Hale dug the money pouch out of his pocket and threw it at Ren.

"There's your damn money back, Ren. Now, are you backing my play?"

"Settle down, Tom. I never said we wouldn't help you. I only wanted to settle things about the money."

"All right, then. It's settled."

Ren nodded. "You can bunk here tonight, and we'll all ride in together before daylight. I expect Murphy intends to cut the Flying X cows out of the herd in the morning. We'll take him outside the livery when he comes for his horse."

"Agreed."

Marion Franks had listened to the entire conversation between Hale and Ren. He couldn't feature a man like Murphy, with his reputation, doing anything of the sort that Hale had described. Murphy sure hadn't seemed the least bothered about facing down six armed men when he and that Mexican woman had ridden into their camp. Franks felt sure Murphy was no coward. He wasn't so sure that was true about Hale, though, now that he considered it.

Things had already grown a lot hotter around Comanche Gap than Franks felt comfortable with. He had already considered leaving the gang and hauling his freight before this had happened. Now Ren planned to make them all tackle Ian Murphy again. Franks didn't like that idea one bit. He figured he'd sooner face a grizzly bear with a jack knife than the business end of Ian Murphy's Colt. Sure, he'd ride into town with them in the morning, but soon as he got the chance, he was pulling stakes and slipping out of town. He wanted no part of Ian Murphy or doing the biding of Tom Hale either, for that matter. And once Murphy took back the Flying X cows, which Franks figured he eventually would, Ren would have to give Logan's money back and they would have nothing left to split, anyway. Yes, the mother of Marion Franks had raised no foolish children, and he was hauling his freight out of Comanche Gap the first chance he got.

# Chapter Thirteen
## Unexpected Warning

WHEN HE WOKE UP the following morning, Murphy left his room for the dining room to have breakfast. There he found Maria Espinosa, already seated at a table eating, wearing her riding outfit. While she still seemed angry with him, it also seemed she intended to go through with buying Colonel Ward's steers. Perhaps she felt she had no other option since her father needed cattle to fulfill the government contract. Murphy removed his hat and sat down across from her. Harry Fisher brought him a plate filled with beef, beans, and biscuits and then filled his coffee cup.

"I waited until after eight to draw the bath you asked for," Fisher said. "But when you didn't show up, I gave up and went to bed."

"That's all right, ma'am," Murphy said. "I didn't get in until late and didn't expect you to stay up all night."

Fisher nodded and left the room for the kitchen.

Espinosa regarded him coldly. "I understand they found those men dead behind the cantina this morning," she said. "It seems they were hanged."

"Those who take to the outlaw trail generally end up at the end of a rope," Murphy said.

"And yet they have not yet hanged you, Señor Murphy," Espinosa replied frostily.

"No," Murphy said. "Perhaps because I'm not an outlaw."

"You killed those men," Espinosa hissed.

"Where there is no law, honorable men do what they must when justice is required."

Espinosa tossed her raven hair angrily and sipped her coffee without making a reply.

"Am I to assume you still plan to buy the steers?" Murphy said.

"I have no choice," Espinosa said. "My father needs cattle to fulfill the contract I spoke of yesterday."

Murphy nodded, wolfing down his breakfast.

The front door opened and a young man, his clothes covered in trail dust, walked in, his spurs jingling. Recognizing the man, Murphy's hand went to his Colt. Noticing the movement, the man raised his hands.

"I'm only here to talk, Murphy," he said. "I got something you'll want to hear."

The man removed his hat, nodded to Espinosa, and sat down on the bench beside her a respectable distance away.

"You were at Ren's camp when we cut the herd," Murphy said.

"Yes sir, I was," the man said. "Marion Franks is my name. I was with Ren and the others, but I'm pulling my stakes and hauling my freight out of Comanche Gap. Yeah, I helped steal them Flying X cows, but I'm no gunslick and smart enough to know it."

"You expecting a fight, Franks?"

"Not me, but the others are. Tom Hale showed up at the camp late last night, mad as a wet hen. He claimed you got the drop on him, disarmed him, and ran him out of town. He says you wouldn't fight him fair. That didn't set right with me."

"So?"

"So Hale talked Ren into helping him kill you. So we all rode into town early this morning. After I got the chance to ask some fella in town about you and Hale, I got the straight story. He backed down. Anyway, Hale, Ren, and the boys are layin' for you, waiting for you to show yourself so they can cut you down. I wanted no part of it. So, I moseyed over to let you know what's what."

"That's mighty neighborly of you."

"Well, the way I see it, what they're plannin' is no different from backshootin' a fella. And a man, even a cow thief, has to draw the line somewhere."

Murphy nodded. "Appreciate it. Where are they?"

"They've got a lookout or two out front, and most of the others are down around the livery waitin' for you to come for your horse. They figure you plan to cut the Flying X cows out of the herd this morning."

"Sounds like I'm afoot then."

"Well, you might be, except I sort of slipped over the back way and happened to bring along your horse. It's tied out back."

"I appreciate that even more."

Franks nodded. "You seem like a good fella and all, but I ain't hankerin' to get myself killed. And I'm no great shakes with a gun, so I'd not be much of a help to you, anyway."

"That's all right," Murphy said. "I'm obliged to you for what you've done already and don't begrudge you taking care of your own business."

"Thanks," Franks said, getting up from the table. "I'll be driftin' then. Good luck to you, Mister Murphy."

Murphy stood up and offered his hand. "Thanks again, and good luck to you, cowboy. And you can call me Ian."

Franks grinned. The men shook hands, then Franks put on his hat and left out the front door.

"Do you think it's a trap?" Espinosa said in alarm.

"No, I believed him," Murphy said. "And I'll believe him even more if I find my horse tied up out back."

"I'll go to the livery for my horse and meet you at the camp of my vaqueros."

"You'll do no such thing," Murphy said.

The harshness of his reply startled her. She opened her mouth to argue, but before she could speak, Murphy spoke abruptly, almost brutally.

"They don't want those Flying X cattle cut out of the herd. They might not kill you, but they would capture you if they got the chance and then use you to get to me."

"But—"

"No," he said firmly in a tone that brooked no argument. "Lock yourself in your room with your pistol close at hand. I plan to lead them out of town on a chase. Then you can get your horse and ride to the spring for you vaqueros. There should be no one on the range with the herd. Take your men and round up the Flying X cattle and start them toward New Mexico Territory. I'll catch up later and we'll settle up then."

"Very well, Ian."

Murphy nodded. After returning to his room for his rifle and canteen, he left the adobe out the back and found his saddled horse waiting. After shoving the Henry rifle into the saddle boot, Murphy climbed aboard the long-legged roan. When he walked the horse around the adobe to the front, he quickly spied the lookout. The man standing in the shadows on the boardwalk across the street from the boarding house leaned against a post, watching the front door of the adobe so intently, he didn't even notice the horse and rider. Murphy drew the Colt and sent a bullet into the post, sending wood splinters flying. The man cried out, then he glanced directly at Murphy and started shouting the alarm. The roan reared as Murphy reined it abruptly around to face the opposite direction and then he spurred the animal and the roan shot up the street toward the gap and the badlands beyond.

# Chapter Fourteen

## Hot Pursuit

THE BIG, LONG-LEGGED, SLAB-SIDED red roan was a splendid traveler. Murphy rode fast into the badlands, the hot, dry, desolate country that was part of the Staked Plains. Folklore said the Spanish explorers, finding the country difficult to navigate because of the lack of distinguishable features, drove stakes into the ground so they could find their way back out again, hence the name. The area became the lair of the Kiowa and Comanches who used it as a sanctuary until their defeat in the 1870s.

It had taken the pursuers time to catch up and mount their horses after Murphy rode out of town, and that, along with the speed of the roan, had given him a good head start. Within a few hours after they took up the pursuit, Murphy, lying on his belly on the bank of an arroyo, studied them carefully through a field glass he carried in his saddlebags. The makeup of the crew following him was Hale, Ren, and four others. The pursuers had brought no pack animals or canvas water bags with them, a sign they expected a short campaign. If they wanted to hunt him, Murphy intended to make certain they grew damn sick of it.

At once, he had struck east into the loneliest, most desolate country imaginable. If they wanted a hunt, he'd give it to them. This was a game he knew well, and there was no trick of white men or the Comanche that had inhabited these plains he did not know. Then he turned south for a while as the sun blazed down from the hot coppery sky. He struck out across the sage brush where the rattlers coiled and buzzards floated high above on the thermal currents. Then he rode west and north, leading his pursuers farther into the desert lands and away from any settlements. He left a trail they could follow, but frequently confused it by doubling back and riding over previous trails at intersecting angles.

The horizon shimmered and became lost in the haze of heat. Above, the soaring buzzards were the only movement to be seen. The sun baked down on upon the desert and the surface threw back the heat in the face like that of a fiery furnace. The faces of the pursuers grew dusty and their throats parched and riding on and on, Murphy checked his back trail and saw the distant cloud of dust, chuckling. Behind him, his pursuers sweated and cursed. Tempers grew short, and the men began hating the sun, the land, and each other.

Murphy had crossed these plains many times with the herds of Goodnight and Loving. He didn't know the land as well as had the Kiowa and Comanche, but he still recalled the locations of the few and widely scattered water holes he knew about. As dusk fell, he paused at a small spring a man might easily have missed had he not known where to find it. There, he unsaddled the horse and allowed it to rest and drink its fill while he ate a supper of cold biscuits and salted, dried beef he had brought from the boarding house kitchen.

Once full darkness had descended, Murphy took up the field glass again and scanned the plains through it. Quickly, he found the blazing fire that marked his pursuers' camp. He would doze for a while and then pay them a visit.

AFTER A FULL DAY riding through what felt like a blast furnace, following the trail that led them deeper and deeper into one of the most awful lands on the face of God's earth, Ren had persuaded Hale to stop and camp for the night. The men gathered what wood they could find to build a fire to brew coffee and cook their supper. Two of Ren's rustlers stretched a lariat between two shrub trees and then tied up the horses to the rope for the night.

"Lord almighty," Ren said to Hale. "We must be over twenty miles from Comanche Gap, right out in the middle of hell."

"He's in as bad a shape as we are after riding in the heat all day," Hale said. "We'll catch up with Murphy sometime tomorrow."

"I'm not so sure we'll catch him at all," Ren said. "He's leadin' us around in a big circle, but taking us farther and farther out into these plains. By noon tomorrow, unless we stumble across a water hole, our canteens will be empty. I say if we don't catch up to him by then, we turn around and head back."

"We're not going back until we run Murphy to ground," Hale said vehemently. "Not until we've filled his hide full of lead."

Ren shook his head. He already knew it had been a mistake to chase Murphy out into these badlands and now he had a terrible feeling about it. He felt sure Murphy had lured them here into this hot, dry, desolate country in hopes they would perish. Or maybe where he could kill them one by one from a distance. But he kept his opinions to himself given the way Hale had snarled and grown more vicious as the day had progressed.

After they had eaten and taken careful swallows of the precious supply of water remaining in their canteens, Ren organized the watch for the night, and then all but Jake Steele, who had drawn the first watch, curled up in their bedrolls to get some sleep. Steel sat facing the fire, unsure what direction he faced and figuring it didn't matter, anyway. Soon, half asleep, his head began nodding.

⁓𝓮𝓵𝓮⁓

AT AROUND THREE IN the morning, Murphy washed his face in the spring water, saddled the roan and remounted. Then he headed the horse at a walk toward the distant fire. Stopping far enough so that the outlaw's horses wouldn't detect the roan and nicker, Murphy continued on foot. He squatted and watched the lone guard by the fire for a while until satisfied the man had fallen asleep. Then Murphy crept silently into the camp. There he dropped to his hands and knees, crawling from bedroll to bedroll, collecting canteens. He then quietly withdrew with all the canteens except that of the guard sitting asleep beside the fire. When he got to the rope where the horses were picketed, Murphy untied them all. Then he led them away.

Once he reached his own horse, Murphy mounted the roan. Then he pulled the Colt and discharged it several times over the heads of the outlaw's horses. Immediately, they wheeled away at a dead run. Murphy turned, slapped his spurs to the roan, and galloped away, satisfied the outlaw's horses likely wouldn't stop until they arrived back at Comanche Gap. He'd put his pursuers afoot in the middle of a hot, dry, desolate country with only one canteen between the group of six men. They had wanted to hunt him. Murphy felt sure they would be damn well sick of it by the middle of their second day on foot, with no water beneath the cloudless skies and the unforgiving sun.

# Chapter Fifteen

## Chaos

THE GUNFIRE WOKE THE startled outlaws, and they rolled out of their bedrolls. A few men, half asleep, drew their pistols and fired wildly into the surrounding darkness until Baldwin Ren got them under control. Hearing nothing else after holstering their guns, they all assembled around the campfire.

"Who was on watch!" cried Hale.

"Steele had the first watch," Ren volunteered when no one answered.

Hale braced Steele, who stood beside the fire with a sheepish expression on his face.

"Did you see anything?"

"No, nothing," Steele said. "Same as you fellas. I heard some gunshots out there somewhere."

"Just that damn Murphy trying to spook us," someone said.

Then some of the men drifted back toward their bedrolls.

"Were you asleep on watch?" Hale demanded of Steele.

Ren looked at his pocket watch is the light of the fire. "It's going on four in the mornin'," he said. "Didn't you wake up your relief?"

"I was about to," Steele lied. "I thought I'd let Burt catch an extra hour of sleep."

"You're lying, damn you," Hale cried, shoving Steele in the chest. "You fell asleep and Murphy walked in on us. He could have killed us all in our sleep."

Suddenly, some cried out. "My canteen is gone. Who took it? That's not funny, damn you."

"Hey," said another. "Mine is missing too. I left it hooked on my saddle horn."

Hale and Ren hurried back to their bedrolls while the others checked for their canteens. All were missing.

"He walked right into our camp and took all the canteens!" Hale said.

"Hey!" a man shouted. "The horses are gone."

"What!" cried Ren. He ran to the picket line and sure enough, all the horses tied there were gone.

The camp erupted into chaos, with everyone shouting at once. Then Hale shoved someone out of his way and made for Steele, now cowering by the fire.

"This is your fault!" cried Hale. "Because you couldn't stay awake. Now we're all afoot out here in this wilderness with no water!"

"He still has his canteen!" someone shouted.

Hale looked at Steele and saw his canteen still hung at his side from the strap over his shoulder.

"Give me the canteen!" he demanded. "You let Murphy walk up on us and take ours. Now we're going to share the water in your canteen and you will do without."

Steele took a step back, shaking his head. "I'm not giving you my canteen, Hale."

Hale gave him a cruel stare, and an evil smile appeared on his lips. "Then you better yank that pistol, because if you don't hand over that canteen, I'll gut shoot you and leave you here to die."

Steele stood trembling, staring at Hale open-mouthed. Then, suddenly, he turned and ran. Hale calmly pulled his pistol, thumbed back the hammer, and shot Steele in the back. Steele pitched forward on his face. Hale strode his lifeless body and yanked the canteen off Steele's shoulder. Then, holstering the Colt, he strutted back to the fire, holding the canteen above his head in triumph.

Ren looked in horror at Steele's body on the ground, and then back at the smiling Hale.

"That was real smart, Tom," Ren said after a moment. "You killed the canteen, too."

"What?" Hale exclaimed, examining the canteen. Then he saw the hole where the bullet had passed through the canteen before killing Steele. It was now empty.

"You shot Steele in the back," someone said.

Hale dropped the canteen, whirled, and grabbed for his gun. But he stopped when he saw Burt McMullin walking toward him with his pistol pointed at Hale's face.

"Don't do anything crazy, Burt," Ren pleaded. "Everyone is worked up. We should all calm down."

But before Ren got the last word out, McMullin squeezed the trigger and shot Tom Hale, the celebrated gunman, in the forehead. Hale was dead before he hit the ground.

"Lord almighty, Burt," Ren said. "You just killed Tom Hale."

UNKNOWN TO THE FOUR men standing beside the fire staring down at the recently departed Tom Hale, Murphy was riding back towards Comanche Gap with the roan at an easy trot. Five canteens plus his own hung from his saddle horn. Murphy had heard a flurry of gunfire riding away from the camp. But he knew the spooked outlaws had been firing wildly into the darkness because none of the bullets had come in his direction. Then minutes later, he'd heard another single gunshot. A couple of minutes later, he'd heard another single shot. A wry grin appeared on Murphy's lips. It seemed the hunters were already killing each other over the one remaining canteen.

# Chapter Sixteen

## The Double Diamond

AFTER RIDING ALL NIGHT, Murphy arrived on the Double Diamond spread around noon. He had ridden directly to the camp where he'd confronted the rustlers since that's where the cattle herd had last been. He found no cattle, but saw from the tracks the direction someone had driven them from the range. The tracks led west towards the Pecos, so Murphy felt sure Maria Espinosa and her vaqueros had rounded up the Flying X steers and were hazing them toward Fort Sumner. Murphy saw something else of interest. A grizzled old cowboy, thin as a rail, standing next to a mound of freshly turned earth, leaning on a shovel and studying him from beneath the brim of a sweat stained, high-crowned hat. Murphy walked the roan over to the man.

"Howdy," said the cowboy.

"Howdy," Murphy said. "It's a mite hot out for digging holes."

"Yes, sir, it sure is. But the dead need burying."

"Who died?"

"Frank Logan," the cowboy said. "He owned this spread. I'm Will Handy, the foreman."

"What happened?"

"Logan pointed a Winchester at the wrong fella. While he was pointing and jawing at the hombre, I'll be damned if the fella didn't shoot him dead center in the chest. He fell down dead right here on this spot."

"You see it?"

"Yes, sir, I did. Logan came to the bunkhouse shouting about someone stealing cows. He made me ride out here with him and we found some vaqueros and a Mexican woman rounding up steers. Logan was madder than I ever recall seeing him. He jerked his Winchester, and the woman rode over to talk to him. Then all hell broke loose."

"You said a fella shot Logan."

"Yep, sure did. Logan was shouting and cursing the woman like nobody's business, and this big fella wearing a red sash around his waist took exception to it I guess. He rode up and Logan swung the Winchester in his direction and cussed him. So, the fella jerked his pistol cool as you please, and shot him dead."

"I guess you stayed above the fray since you're not getting buried."

Handy grinned, took off his hat, and mopped the sweat from his bald head with a bandana.

"Well, I never figured on getting killed over a bunch of cows, especially stolen cows. I warned Logan it was a bad idea to buy stolen stock from a bunch of known rustlers. Sounded to me like the woman and her vaqueros were just taking them back for the rightful owner."

"That's exactly what they were doing," Murphy said. "Those steers belonged to a Fort Stockton rancher I work for. I sold the steers to the woman to save driving them back to the ranch."

"Well, I feel a sight better about things since I know the whole story," Handy said. "I've always tried to ride for the brand, but I never was a gun hand anyhow."

"Why are you burying Logan out here? Isn't there a graveyard hereabouts?"

"Well, I never liked Logan much, anyway. Seemed a sight easier to plant him here than hauling him somewhere else. I doubt it makes much difference to him."

Murphy laughed. "I guess you have a point there."

"Was Logan a friend of yours?" Handy asked.

"No, I only stopped by to kill him," Murphy said evenly. "He paid a fella named Tom Hale to kill a friend of mine to cover up buying those stolen steers. So, I guess that vaquero wearing the red sash saved me some trouble."

Handy nodded. "I told Logan buying that stolen stock was a bad idea."

***

As EAGER AS HE was to catch up with the herd and especially to see Maria Espinosa again, Murphy knew he needed sleep before taking the trail again after riding all night. So, he rode into Comanche Gap, where he found the main street empty and still, even though it was early afternoon. After leaving the roan in the care of the young stable hand at the livery, Murphy went to the boarding house.

After Harry Fisher brought him a plate of food, she heated water in the kitchen for Murphy's long delayed bath. After scrubbing off the trail dust and soaking until the water had tuned cool, Murphy went to his room, stretched out on the bed, and promptly fell asleep.

AFTER LEAVING THE DOUBLE Diamond range, Maria Espinosa and her nine vaqueros pushed the Flying X steers west along an established trail among the scrub and ocotillo to Horsehead Crossing. Here at the Pecos River, after watering the cattle, they turned the herd north toward New Mexico Territory and Fort Sumner more than two hundred miles away. Espinosa rode in silence beside Antonio Montoya. They were mostly past the heated argument that erupted after Antonio had killed Frank Logan. Espinosa, who viewed violence as a last resort to be used only when all else had failed, felt her segundo had shown poor judgement by resorting to killing too quickly. Montoya had patiently explained the gringo was out of his head with anger, and waving his rifle around wildly, he might have, perhaps even unintentionally, killed her. Montoya stubbornly insisted he had been unwilling to take that risk.

Only one day and night out of Comanche Gap, Espinosa already turned frequently in her saddle, wistfully checking the back trail. Concern for his welfare had long since supplanted her anger with Ian Murphy. She wanted nothing more than to see him overtaking the herd, safe and sound.

"Jefe, you must prepare yourself for the worst," Montoya said, sensing why she looked back so often. "Six men pursued him. He may no longer live."

"I don't believe he is dead," Espinosa said. "I think I would feel it if that were true."

Montoya shook his head. "Jefe, with all respect, you hardly know the man."

"I know enough," Espinosa said stubbornly. "Despite being too quick, like you, Antonio, to resort to violence, he is a good man."

"Perhaps," Montoya said, unwilling to get drawn into another bitter argument.

# Chapter Seventeen

## The Herd

THROUGH THE DOWN-POINTED FIELD glass, Murphy's gaze inched from right to left along the trail that twisted along within sight of the river. Then, peering intently through the glass into the dust cloud, he made out the plodding steers and the riders. Where he sat in the saddle aboard the long-legged red roan, the ground dropped slightly away from him in a long, sweep of short grass. The glass moved left again and Murphy's breath caught for a moment when he saw her, sitting tall and straight in the saddle on the paint horse, every inch a desirable woman. For several moments, Murphy watched her, then slipped the glass into a saddlebag, spurred his mount lightly, and slanted down the slope to the trail. The fact was, everything felt good. It was good to have overtaken the herd and good to see the things there were to see. It was going to be good to see her up close and to look into her brown eyes again.

Maria Espinosa turned to check the back trail again, perhaps for the twentieth time in the past hour. Her breath quickened when she thought she saw an approaching horse and rider back there in the dust cloud. She lifted the brim of her hat and shaded her eyes with both hands, and then she was sure her eyes hadn't deceived her. Tugging the hat back down, Maria Espinosa reined the paint tightly, and after it turned, she spurred the horse eagerly and galloped away from the herd. Startled, when he saw Espinosa wheel her horse around and gallop back the way they had come, Antonio Montoya started to follow, but then with sad eyes saw where she was riding off to, or to who.

Murphy couldn't wipe the grin off his face as he watched her riding toward him. He spurred the roan into a canter to close the distance quicker. When they met, they both reined their mounts to a halt. Murphy climbed down while Maria leaped to the ground from her saddle. She jerked the bandana covering her face down, revealing a wide smile, as she hurried toward him. Murphy stood waiting for her to speak so he might determine if she was still upset with him. But to his surprise, she neither spoke nor stopped until she reached him. Then, to his astonishment, Maria Espinosa threw herself into his arms, knocking his hat askew, and then she pressed her full lips to his.

After the unexpected kiss, Maria took off her hat and rested her head on his shoulder.

"Gracias a Dios!" she cried. "You're safe. I was so worried!"

Murphy stood self-consciously, holding her in his arms in astonishment. He cleared his throat before saying, "They never even got close to me. I'm fine and so glad to see you again. It's all over now."

Maria stepped back, but grasped his hands in hers. With lips parted, her eyes held him with astonishment—the dark eyes that looked almost black, and her face, warm brown against the whiteness of her shirt.

Her eyes narrowed as she studied him. "It's over? Did you kill them all?"

"Nope, not exactly. I only left them afoot, without water in a mighty hot place. I gave them a chance, not much of one, but more of a chance than any of them deserved."

"Well, at least you didn't shoot them. That's good at least, I suppose."

Murphy nodded.

She smiled at him. "You're staying with us for a while?"

"Well, maybe a little while."

"You could ride with us to Fort Sumner," Maria said. "I could introduce you to my father, Don Pablo."

"I'd like that," Murphy said. "I really would. But, I can't this time. I have business back in Comanche Gap to attend to."

"But you said it's over. What more is there you must do?"

Murphy explained how the old prospector, Charlie Henry, had approached him with a business proposition. And about the gold and silver, Emperor Maximilian's treasure Henry had found.

"He offered me five thousand dollars to help him haul a load of gold and silver to the bank in Odessa. It shouldn't take more than a few days."

Maria's eyes widened. "What will you do with so much money?"

Murphy smiled. "I'll buy me a little ranch somewhere and raise a few cows and some horses of my own. It's something I've wanted to do for a long time."

Maria frowned suddenly. "So, you came only to get the money for the cattle?" she said. "Then you will ride away?" Her tone suggested hurt feelings.

"Of course not," Murphy said shyly. "I came because I wanted to see you."

Noticing the shyness, she smiled at him, laughing a little. "Tough, aren't you? So big and tough. But under all that, you're sentimental as a little boy. And you care for me. I've known since the day we met."

"Well," Murphy, stammered. "Of course I care for you, Maria."

She stepped forward and embraced him again. And he kissed her, so sure of himself, she almost laughed. Then he let go and stepped back as if to say there, now you've been kissed and you won't ever doubt that I care for you.

"Hey," Murphy said, breaking the spell. We better catch up to the herd.

"Will you stay with us? A few days, at least? Please, Ian?"

"I'll stay for a while," Murphy said. "But I must return to Comanche Gap tomorrow."

Her pouty lips showed her disappointment.

"But once I've finished the job for old Charlie Henry, I should catch up to you again before you're back in Fort Sumner. So, you can still introduce me to your father, if you're of a mind to."

Maria brightened. "That's all right then, I suppose."

Then they mounted their horses and rode after the herd.

WHEN THE HERD REACHED the night's camp that Antonio had selected, the vaqueros bedded them down to rest, graze, and water. After setting the first watch, the rest of the vaqueros descended upon the chuck wagon that had traveled ahead of the herd. The cook served up plates or beans, pan de campo, a type of bread cooked in a skillet, and coffee, simple fare but filling.

After supper, some vaqueros took to their bedrolls after a long day in the saddle. Others gathered around the campfire, talking quietly so as not to spook the cattle while one played a guitar softly. As Murphy sat on the ground beside Maria near the fire, he caught Antonio glaring at him. The man seemed to resent his presence. Murphy figured her segundo, obviously protective of her, didn't trust him. Or perhaps the man had feelings for Maria himself and considered Murphy a rival. After a while, Maria touched his knee and pointed towards a small grove of trees near the river.

"It might be cooler there for sleeping," she said innocently. "Perhaps we should take our bedrolls there."

"Just you and me?" Murphy asked in astonishment.

"Yes," she said, chuckling.

"All right, I guess," Murphy said.

They got up, and Murphy grabbed his bedroll from his saddle while Maria collected hers from the wagon. Together, they strolled to the grove.

"Seems you were right," Murphy said as they fixed their bedrolls on the ground in the spot Maria chose where the trees screened them from view from the camp. "There's a pleasant breeze coming across the water."

Maria looked at him and smiled.

"You're so beautiful it hurts," Murphy blurted.

Maria laughed. "Hurts who? Certainly not you, the big tough pistolero."

Lying side by side, Murphy looked at her—her lissome figure, olive skin, and large dark brown eyes. Her wet lips parted slightly, and her eyes widened a little. He saw the sudden hunger in her eyes. Then she reached for him and he took her in his arms and pulled her to him. Hungrily, their lips sought each others and melted together. Something deep welled up within him and the dam holding back his feelings was gone.

Sometime later, she pushed away from him, her breath coming quickly, and his ragged with emotion. She lay on her back beside him, their naked bodies touching. Murphy felt half frightened by the feelings that shook him.

"It's no good, Maria," he said finally. "No good at all. You're too much to waste on a drifter like me. I'm a man who lives by the gun. My time could come next week, next month, even tomorrow."

Maria rolled toward him, her head propped on her elbow.

"I don't care about any of that, Ian Murphy. Since the day we met, I have felt so restless. I know how you have lived. None of that matters. I care nothing about tomorrow, only today. I'm satisfied feeling your arms around me, and with your kisses. Perhaps someday we can have more. I know that's what I want, but I can be realistic."

Then Maria put her fingers to her lips and touched them to his. "Is that asking too much?"

"No, it all sounds mighty fine to me," he said, holding her warm hand against his cheek.

"We might persuade my father to sell you land for your rancho," she said. "He has property apart from his rancho that he has purchased over the years, range we aren't even using. There is water there, and good grass for raising cattle."

"That's something to think about," Murphy said. "I've thought a lot about settling down somewhere people don't know me, somewhere my reputation wouldn't work against me."

"You could have that in Fort Sumner, Ian. And you could have me. If that's what you want."

He gazed at her and tried to find words, but there were none.

# Chapter Eighteen

## More Trouble at the Cantina

IAN MURPHY RODE UPHILL into the east side of Comanche Gap, riding on until he reached the livery. There he dismounted and stabled his horse. He planned on staying in town at the boarding house for the night before meeting Charlie Henry at his camp the following morning. But Murphy didn't walk directly to the boarding house. He headed for the cantina. He wanted to learn if any word of Tom Hale and the Baldwin Ren gang had reached the town. If so, there might be men in the lawless town looking for him since he expected Hale, Ren, and the others likely had friends among the other bandits and no-accounts inhabiting Comanche Gap. Murphy wanted to know whether any with revenge on their minds were huntin' him before he started up the trail with Henry and what the old prospector claimed was a right smart amount of gold and silver. Murphy had no wish to bring trouble with him when he met up with Henry.

Casting a careful glance around the place when he entered the cantina, he saw only a handful of men present. They all sat around tables or stood at the bar drinking, with no one at the poker table. Walt Hansen, behind the bar, looked at Murphy warily as he walked up to the bar.

"What will you have?" asked Hansen, no pretense of friendliness in his tone.

"Whiskey, if you're quick about it," Murphy said sharply. "I'm in a hurry and have no time to waste."

As Hansen slammed a glass on the bar and filled it from a bottle, he sloshed the whiskey on the glass and the bar beside it.

"You drink that one," Murphy said, "and then pour me another in a fresh glass without the mess."

Hansen didn't like it, but after looking into Murphy's hard gray eyes, he picked up the glass and downed the liquor. Then he put a fresh glass on the bar in front of Murphy and filled it, careful not to spill a drop.

"Has Tom Hale been in to claim his guns?" Murphy asked, feigning simple curiosity. Hansen had been behind the bar the night he had faced down Hale and run him out of town.

"I haven't seen Tom since the other night," Hansen said carefully, his surly tone gone from his speech.

"What of Baldwin Ren? Have you seen him lately?"

Hansen shook his head. "What do you want with Ren? I didn't know you knew him."

"I know him."

"Anything else?" Hansen said.

"No," said Murphy, sipping the whiskey.

Hansen nodded, and then turned and went through a door behind the bar into a back room. Murphy knew Hansen had seen neither Hale nor Ren before he asked, because he knew where they were, if they were still alive. In that, Hansen had told the truth, but Murphy had sensed the man was holding something back.

He turned to scan the room for Joe Merritt, a man he'd met in the cantina the day he first arrived in Comanche Gap. Merritt, it seemed, knew all the town gossip. Maybe he'd heard something about Hale and Ren. Murphy expected at least some of the riderless horses he'd run off in the desert had made it back to the town by now.

While he didn't see Merritt, he saw someone he recognized, Wes Boudin, a gambler he'd once met in Abilene back during the wild days when he'd gone up the trails from Texas with the Longhorn herds. Boudin, who had once been a faro dealer at the Alamo, the most elaborate of the Abilene saloons, had been more than a card shark. He had also made a name for himself as a gunman up in Kansas, although Murphy had never quarreled with him. Boudin sat alone at a table playing solitaire, paying Murphy no mind.

As he turned and finished the drink, the door behind the bar opened and Hansen followed another man out of the back room, a slope-shouldered man with dark hair and eyes who walked with a noticeable limp. Hansen stayed back behind the bar, but the other man stepped awkwardly around the bar and walked toward Murphy. The limp triggered some distant memory for Murphy, but he couldn't immediately get a firm grip on it.

"So, you're Murphy?" the man said brusquely.

"Might be," Murphy said. "Who's asking?"

"Otto Schmidt. I own this place and I run this town."

Schmidt was a man in his forties, as tall as Murphy, and only a little bulkier.

"Well, congratulation, but it ain't much of a saloon or a town far as I can tell," Murphy said, in response to the man's arrogant demeanor.

"Where's Tom Hale?" Schmidt demanded, ignoring Murphy's insult.

"How would I know? It's not my day to keep up with Hale."

"His horse came in yesterday without him and without a saddle," Schmidt said. "I heard about the trouble you started in here the other night."

Sensing movement to his right, Murphy glanced toward Boudin. He saw Boudin now looked directly at him and had tuned his chair to face him with his cards now all laying on the table. Boudin's short jacket was open, revealing the butt of a revolver in a cross-draw holster. The rising tensions in the room spelled trouble brewing, and Murphy grew wary, knowing such currents could spell death for a man without his instincts. He turned back to face Schmidt.

"I wouldn't know anything about Hale losing his horse," Murphy said. "Sounds pretty careless of him, losing his horse like that while he's out hunting in the badlands."

Schmidt's face flushed red. "Murphy, I want you out of town by sundown today. Ride on, keep riding, and don't come back."

Murphy grinned. "Far as I know, no saloon keeper has any authority to run a man out of town. I suppose I'll leave when I get ready."

Schmidt started, and then glanced at Boudin, his face even redder. He edged closer along the bar, undisguised contempt in eyes. Murphy waited. He knew the man had not expected him to leave town on his order. This would be a killing for one or the other, but he'd give Schmidt the chance to make the first play.

"You'll leave like I told you," Schmidt snarled, "or they will carry you out in a box."

Murphy knew inside of him, Schmidt was poised for the kill, and Boudin would back his play. He wanted to startle Schmidt, unnerve him and throw him off balance. He took a step forward.

"Is that so? Murphy said, striking quickly with his left hand as he spoke, slapping Schmidt across the mouth. It was a powerful slap that shocked Schmidt and sent him reeling.

Men dived for cover, falling over splintering chairs and overturning tables. Because of the bad leg, Schmidt tripped and sprawled backward onto the floor. Murphy had palmed his Colt with his right hand, in the same motion while striking Schmidt, and stepping to the left, he shot Boudin in the chest who had lunged to his feet and pulled his pistol. Boudin triggered his Colt, as his other hand went to his chest but his bullet went into the floor. In shocked amazement, he stood looking at his bloody hand, as Murphy kept his gun centered on the man for another shot if needed. Then Boudin's legs wilted, and he pitched forward, dropping his gun and clutching at the table. As he fell, the table tipped over, cascading the playing cards over him and the surrounding floor.

Murphy staggered, shaken as if struck by a blow, with no realization of where the blow had come from. He wheeled toward Schmidt, who was sitting on the floor. A sleeve gun had dropped into his hand and he had cut down on Murphy without getting to this feet. Murphy triggered the Colt. Schmidt felt something slap him in the chest as he tried to bring his Remington Double Derringer to bear for a second shot at Murphy. Then he felt a second slap. Suddenly, feeling very weak, he slumped onto his back, staring up at the rafters below the open roof. He could see sunlight through a crack in the roof above, and then the light was gone, and he was dead.

After shooting Schmidt, Murphy spun to face the bar, his Colt pointed at Hansen. Hansen threw up his hands.

"Not me, Murphy!" he cried. "I'm not in it. He made a hell of a life for all of us."

Murphy's mind clicked, and he then remembered. He remembered why the limp had seemed familiar. And he remembered the hideout gun.

"Weren't you in Abilene once?" he asked Hansen. "You ever hang out in the Alamo?"

Hansen's face tightened. "I remember the place," he said.

"So do I," Murphy said. "And I remember you and Otto Schmidt, too. Only he went by the name Jack Lebold when he ran the Alamo. You and Boudin both worked for him back then, too. But I never knew your name."

Hansen nodded. "Yeah, you're right."

Murphy backed out of the cantina, still pointing the Colt, holding it at waist level. His eyes scanned the room. Once outside, he reloaded before holstering the gun, then headed for the boarding house. His hip bone bothered him, and he limped a little as he walked toward the rooming house. He had been aware of it since feeling the blow after shooting Boudin, but it really hurt now. He stopped and looked down and saw two mangled cartridges in slightly torn leather loops on his gun belt. Murphy laughed. Schmidt's bullet had evidently struck and glanced off the two cartridges, damaging them and the loops, and saving him from a bullet wound. But it seemed Schmidt's shot would leave him with a nasty bruise on his hip for a while.

# Chapter Nineteen

## Preparing to Travel

AN HOUR AFTER DAYBREAK, Ian Murphy rode west past the stage station and, once through the one-mile gap, turned northwest in the general direction of the mesa named Castle Mountain on the north side. But he didn't simply follow the route Henry had given him directly because he had no intention of leaving a trail that anyone might easily follow. Along the way, he paused and checked his back trail for anyone who might have followed him from town. Since Henry had come to Murphy's room at the boarding house in the dead of night to offer his proposition, there was no reason to believe anyone knew any connection existed between them. But given the stakes and because he was a careful man by nature, Murphy took no chances.

Because of the roundabout route he took with detours to confuse his trail, Murphy rode over ten miles, getting to Henry's camp when it lay only four miles outside the town of Comanche Gap, little more than two miles from the road that passed through the gap itself used by the stage line.

After locating the last landmark Henry had labeled on the map that the old prospector had given him that Murphy had memorized before burning it, he rode uphill until he arrived where bare rock jutted up from the side of the mesa. Scanning left and right, he saw a shadowed crevice in the rock that looked like the opening to a cave. Scrub and bushes partially concealed it. After dismounting, Murphy walked to the crevice, leading the roan. As he neared it, Charlie Henry poked his head out of the opening behind a pointed Winchester. When he saw Murphy, he cackled and lowered the rifle.

"Sure was hopin' it was you coming," Henry said. "I've heard horseshoes striking stone for the past ten minutes, and didn't expect you for another two or three days."

"I wrapped up my business sooner than expected," Murphy said. "You got a cave back there?"

"More of a hole. It only goes back into the mountain about four feet. But it makes for a good hidey-hole and a dry camp. Come on up."

Murphy led the horse to the opening, loosened the cinch, and left the horse to graze on the short grass. Then he ducked his head and entered the opening. It was more of a natural covered cut into the rock than a cave, wide at ground level and narrow toward the top. Henry's bedroll was along one side and there was a lantern burning on a natural shelf that lighted the interior. Murphy saw about a dozen barrels about the size of horse shoe kegs stacked along the back wall. He could make out the Spanish lettering, *La Harina*, stenciled on the sides of the wooden kegs.

Henry sat on the ground with his back to a wall.

"Have a sit and let's make a plan, young fella," he said.

Murphy sat down carefully, accommodating his sore hip.

"Looks like we'll need more than your burro and my horse to haul all those barrels to Odessa," Murphy said.

Henry chuckled. "Yes, sir. That's for sure. Don't worry. I bought an old freight wagon and two mules from Abernathy at the livery, and he's holding them for me. That's what I was doing there that day that Rex Walker jumped me and you came along."

"I don't see us getting a wagon up here."

"That's not what I had in mind," Henry said with a grin. "Did you see that mesquite thicket off the stage road riding up here?"

"Hard to miss it. It's some of the only trees of any kind around these parts."

Henry nodded. "We'll use Bessie to pack the barrels down there and cache them in the thicket. I'll stay with them while you ride back to town and get the wagon and drive it back. Then we'll pull the wagon in there and load them up."

"Sounds like we have some work ahead of us."

"It won't take that long. Bessie is stout as they come. She can carry two kegs at a time on the pack frame. It'll take us about a half dozen trips."

"Well, we best get to it," Murphy said, standing up. "That sounds like an all-day job to me."

Henry scrambled to his feet and grabbed a pack frame. Murphy started rolling the kegs to the entrance while the old prospector went to get his burro. After Henry returned and strapped the frame to the back of the burro, he and Murphy lifted a keg and set it onto the pack frame on the right side and then another on the left side. Then, with Henry leading the burro, they followed the path he set that took them directly to the mesquite thicket, which was about a mile and a half in a straight line from the camp. They repeated the process again and again. It was after four o'clock in the afternoon when they loaded the last two kegs on the burro.

"You better ride back for the wagon. They close up the livery for the night at six," Henry said. "I can off load these last two all right when I get them to the thicket."

Murphy nodded. "Being up close to that road, you better keep that Winchester handy until I get back," he said.

"Will do, youngster."

Murphy climbed aboard the roan after tightening the cinch and rode back to the stage road. Henry and the burro plodded toward the thicket with the last two barrels and what belongings he was taking with him, leaving all his digging tools behind inside his rock shelter.

～ℓℓ～

MURPHY HURRIED THE ROAN once he struck the stage road, urging the horse into a canter. He wanted to get to the livery before closing, to get the wagon and team to avoid any delay in getting away from Comanche Gap.

When Murphy arrived, Carl Abernathy was in the process of closing up. He turned and watched Murphy climb down from his horse.

"You made it just in time if you're stabling that roan," Abernathy said.

"I'm not leaving my horse this time. I'm here to pick up the wagon and team you're holding for old Henry."

Abernathy's eye widened. "You and Henry working together now?"

"I'm helping him haul some supplies, that's all," Murphy said, unwilling to share the true purpose of the wagon and team. "He's busy, and I offered to come in and get the wagon for him."

"All right," Abernathy said. Turning, he shouted into the barn, "Hey, Jimmy, get that mule team from the corral and hitch them to the old wagon out back!"

"Yes, pa," Jimmy shouted back.

"No offense," Abernathy said to Murphy. "But I'll admit when I heard about them finding those two fellas dead behind the cantina, I didn't agree with how you handled it."

"No offense taken. A man is entitled to his opinion."

"Then I heard about what happened over at the cantina yesterday with Otto Schmidt and his other gun hand."

"You disagree with that, too?"

Abernathy turned and spat tobacco juice on the ground. When he looked back at Murphy, he grinned.

"No, sir, that made me reconsider things, and I've sure changed my mind about things. If the rumors going around about Tom Hale and the Ren gang are also true, it seems like you've about cleaned up this old town in less than a week. You've done the decent folks around here a big service. Maybe now that we've got shut of some of the riff raff, we might make something good of this town."

"I hope so," Murphy said. "But I won't pretend that I did what I did for the town. I had my own reasons for doing what I did."

"Sure, I understand you wanted justice for your friends they killed. But the way she worked out, I think our town came out of it in a lot better shape than we've been in for longer than I can remember."

"Glad to hear it, and I wish you and the others good luck. But you still have a good many bandits hanging around. Comanche Gap would do well to get some law in here while you've got the numbers whittled down a little."

Jimmy came around the corner of the stable barn, leading the team of mules hitched to a weathered old freight wagon.

Murphy led the roan to the back of the wagon and hitched it to the wagon. Walking back to the front, he prepared to climb up to the seat.

Abernathy stepped forward, and after wiping his right hand on his pants, offered it to Murphy.

"Well, I'll be thanking you for what you did here, Mister Murphy."

Murphy grinned, took the liveryman's hand, and they shook. "Appreciate it, but just call me Ian."

Murphy turned, climbed up, and sat down on the seat. Then he reached out and unwound the wrapped reins from the brake lever.

He tipped his hat to Abernathy and the boy, and then, slapping the reins on the backs of the mules, headed back to the gap and out of town.

⁓ℓℓ⁓

CHARLIE HENRY BREATHED A sigh of relief as Murphy reined the team and hauled the wagon to a stop behind the mesquite grove. He had felt uneasy crouching alone in the grove, so close to the stage road, alone with the gold and silver he had painstakingly uncovered with many weeks of labor.

Henry and Murphy loaded the kegs of treasure into the back of the wagon and covered them with a tarp. Darkness had fallen by the time they had finished. Given the lateness of the hour, the men agreed they would have to delay the start for Odessa until the following morning. While Murphy unhitched the team, hobbled the mules, and unsaddled the roan, Henry built a small fire and got busy rustling up some grub from his meager supplies.

After their supper, the men laid out their bedrolls beneath the wagon and drifted into an uneasy sleep.

# Chapter Twenty

## The Journey Begins

SIX MILES TO THE northwest of Comanche Gap, Ian Murphy handled the team as the wagon rumbled along the stage road, with Charlie Henry sitting on the seat beside him. After making an early start from the mesquite grove camp, the men had stopped briefly at the town livery to leave Henry's burro in the corral. The old prospector had arranged previously with Jimmy Abernathy to care for the animal in his absence. Then, at last, they had left the town of Comanche Gap behind them.

"Are you planning to go back later to search for the rest of the treasure?" Murphy said.

"No, I'm not a greedy man," Henry said, puffing on a cigar. "I'm an old man and have more than enough in this wagon to support me for the rest of my life. And who knows whether others might have already found the rest of it? It's been over a dozen years since they buried that treasure, and the stories of it are widely known by now."

"I've heard a little about it," Murphy said. "But I don't know the details."

"Well, we've got nothing but time to pass until we reach Odessa," Henry cackled. "So, allow me to enlighten you."

Henry told Murphy the story of Maximilian's treasure. Knowing his time as emperor was running out, Maximilian wanted to take with him as much of his mountains of gold, silver, and jewels as possible when he fled back to Europe. So, one day in 1866, he sent fifteen wagons north, loaded with treasure disguised as barrels of flour, clandestinely under the guard of a small detachment of Austrian guards. Their orders were to transport the treasure to the port at Galveston, where they would transfer it to a ship bound for Europe.

Soon after crossing the Rio Grande, the four Austrian soldiers guarding the wagon train met six former Confederate soldiers from Missouri bound for Mexico. The men reported Indians and bandits on the road ahead, so the Austrians offered to hire them to help protect the valuable load of "flour" they claimed they were hauling to San Antonio. The Missouri men accepted the job, but soon noticed the overly protective way the Austrians treated the load of flour. That struck them as odd and created suspicions they were helping escort a cargo of something far more valuable than flour. Finally, the men's curiosity reached the point where they had to find out.

One night after the wagon train had stopped to camp, one of the Missourians lifted the canvas on one wagon and pried open a few of the barrels. When he reported to his companions that he had found them full of gold and silver and jewels, they made a plan to steal the treasure.

The following night, when after the caravan camped near a place called Comanche Gap, fifteen miles from Horse Head Crossing on the Pecos River, the Missouri men struck. First, they killed the Austrians and then turned their attention to gunning down the Mexican teamsters as they resisted or attempted to escape. When the slaughter was over, nineteen men lay dead and the former Confederates owned the treasure.

"It seems killing the teamsters was a poor idea," Murphy said. "With only six men, they had no way of driving all the wagons."

"People speculate the teamsters resisted them or refused to cooperate and that forced them to kill them," Henry said. "But you're right. That posed a significant problem. That's why they unloaded the wagons and buried the treasure. After breaking up the wagons and burning them and the corpses they left behind, they continued north with only what gold coins they could carry on their horses. They intended to reach Missouri, organize an expedition, and to return for the rest of the treasure later."

"Then what happened?" Murphy said.

Henry continued the story. Two days later, one man became sick, and dropped out. The rest, assuming he would die, left him behind and rode away. But a few days later, the sick man recovered sufficiently to travel, and he continued on to catch up with the others. But when he overtook them, he came upon the bodies of the other five Missouri men. Ironically, a short time after leaving him for dead, a Comanche raiding party ambushed and killed them. He found their horses gone and their discarded saddlebags empty.

The lone survivor continued on, but by the time he arrived in north Texas had taken seriously ill again and stopped in a town. A doctor there treated him, but he was so badly ill, the Missouri man didn't stand a chance.

His condition went from bad to worse, no matter what the doctor did. Finally, before he died, he told the doctor the complete story and drew a treasure map and gave it to the doctor in return for his kindness.

"The same map you bought?"

"Yep," said Henry. "The doctor organized a group and traveled to Comanche Gap with the map. But they couldn't find or interpret all landmarks on the map. They found no evidence of burned freight wagons or any treasure. Figuring the Missouri man's memory had been faulty because of his illness, or that someone else got to the treasure first, they abandoned the search and returned home. I met that doctor and he told me the story and later sold me the map."

"And you deciphered the map landmarks, succeeding where the doctor failed."

"To some extent. I found what we're hauling back there in this wagon. Perhaps others found the rest or some of it, or it's still buried back there near the gap. But I'm satisfied to have what I've got."

"Are you settling in Odessa when we get there?"

"No, once I've banked the gold and silver, I'll have the bank transfer the money to a bank back east in Maryland, where I'm moving to live out the rest of my days. I have two daughters living back there in Baltimore. What about you youngster? What will you do with the five thousand you're earning?"

"I'll buy me a little spread somewhere, maybe in New Mexico Territory, if some things work out right for me. Then I'll raise horses and run a few cows to make my living."

The men continued traveling all day, stopping only for brief periods to rest and water the stock before pushing on. By three in the afternoon, they had crossed the Pecos River at the shallow ford of Horsehead Crossing. Then, four hours later, they stopped and made camp for the night at an abandoned homestead with a good well, still some twenty miles south of their destination.

Inside the tumble-down house, they found signs of recent habitation, but it didn't appear anyone permanently occupied the place any longer. Murphy unhitched the team and they drew water from the well for the stock before leaving them to graze on the grass in the yard inside the limestone walls surrounding the place.

After a supper of beef jerky and coffee, the men laid out their bedrolls on the floor to sleep.

# Chapter Twenty-One

## Bandits

THE FIRST RAYS OF sunlight were shining through the shack's lone window when Murphy heard the roan whinny outside, the sound a horse makes as a greeting to other horses. Hurriedly, Murphy pulled on his boots and then standing, strapped on his gun belt.

Henry, awake now too, looked around and sat up.

"What is it?" he asked.

"Someone's coming," Murphy said, striding to the door. "The roan has detected other horses nearby."

Watching from the doorway, Murphy saw four riders galloping their mounts toward the homestead. He watched as they pulled up inside the limestone walls and dismounted. One had thrown down a strong box before getting off his horse, the type he recognized as those carried aboard stage coaches. The men gathered around the wagon.

"Looks like outlaws," Murphy said to Henry. "Better grab your Winchester and keep it handy." Then he stepped outside onto the dilapidated porch.

Hearing the jingle of Murphy's spurs, the men turned toward him as he approached them.

"Who might you be?" a grim, hard-bitten man wearing a red shirt asked. "You're squatting in our place."

"Sorry friend," Murphy said amicably. "I thought it abandoned and only stopped to pass the night."

"What's in the wagon?" the red-shirted man said.

"That's my business, friend," Murphy said. "Nobody else's."

The red-shirted man didn't respond, and Murphy saw the indecision on his face. The man had liked no part of what he'd said, but apparently couldn't decide on a course of action.

"You look little like any freighter I've ever seen," said another, a thin-legged man with a long, loose jaw. He watched Murphy with watery blue eyes.

"Maybe you stole this here wagon," said a lean, wide-shouldered man with smoky eyes and a darkly tanned face. "Maybe we better have a look under that tarp."

"I wouldn't advise it," Murphy said casually.

"No teamster I ever heard of tows a horse behind a freight wagon," red shirt said, jerking his head toward the roan. "I expect we have as much right to whatever is in that wagon as you."

"Well then, if you aim to help yourself, you'll have to get past me first," Murphy said. "But if I were you fellas, I'd take your Wells Fargo strong box over there and ride out of here until I've hitched my team and am on my way. In the meantime, shuck those gun belts so we can avoid any misunderstandings. You can collect them later, after I've gone."

The fourth man, bearded and wearing a low-crowned, stiff-brimmed hat, stepped out in front.

"You're powerful sure of yourself considering you're looking at long odds," the man said. "Looks like four to one to me, stranger."

"Maybe the odds aren't as long as you think," Murphy said. "Maybe I have a friend inside the house there with a Winchester pointed at you."

The man hesitated, his right hand near his belted gun.

"Maybe we should take his suggestion, Brady," said the man wearing the red shirt. "I don't care for the looks of this fella, and he seems too damn sure of himself."

"You scared, Ed?" the man called Brady snickered. "You sayin' we ought to let this one fella put the run on us?"

"He might have a load of dry goods in that wagon for all we know," Ed said. "I don't see that's worth anybody gettin' killed over."

"I'm not much for talkin'," Murphy said coldly to the bearded man. "Either shuck the gun belts and fork your horses and ride or make your play. I need to be on my way, and you're wasting my time."

"We can't do that," Brady said.

"You don't know what you can do till you try," Murphy said flatly.

Brady flinched and then palmed his pistol, but before he cleared leather, there came the deafening report of Murphy's Colt. Brady went down, clutching his middle. As Murphy pivoted left, and shot the lean, wide-shouldered man in the chest, a Winchester inside the doorway of the shack whined and the rifle bullet sent the thin-legged man down flat on his back with a red stain blossoming on the front of his shirt. When the shooting started, Ed, the red-shirted man, had turned and run to his horse. When Murphy turned his way, Ed was already spurring his horse out through the opening between the limestone walls. The Winchester whined again, and throwing up his hands, Ed tumbled out of the saddle and hit the dirt.

As Murphy checked the three downed men in the yard with the toe of his boot, Henry joined him.

"Are they all dead?" he said.

"These three are," Murphy said. "I'm rarely in agreement with shooting a man in the back, but in this case, I agree you had to do it. If he'd gotten away, he might have set others on us."

"That was my thinking. You braced them before I could get to the door with the Winchester. I wasn't sure if they had already looked under the tarp. I feared if the man knew what we had, he might have been riding to get someone to help rob us on down the trail."

"They didn't get the chance to look, but I understand your thinking."

Henry nodded and walked over to the strong box on the ground. "It's a Wells Fargo box," he said.

"Figured it."

"Reckon we should take it along?"

"No, if we run into a lawman, I don't want to explain where we got property belonging to Wells Fargo. We'll hide it somewhere on the place and you can report its whereabouts to the law in Odessa if you're a mind to.

—ele—

AROUND NOON, NINE RIDERS cut the stage road, and the lead rider signaled Murphy to stop.

"Dad blame it," Henry swore, levering a bullet into the chamber of his rifle. "More bandits?"

Murphy put a hand on the rifle barrel and pushed it down.

"Hold on, old timer," he said. "That gent at the front is wearing a star on his shirt. It looks like a posse."

After Murphy halted the team, the riders walked their horses forward and stopped beside the wagon box.

"I'm Bill Cole, out of Tom Green County," the lead horseman said. "You men see four fellas riding south in a hurry? One of them wearing a

bright red shirt?"

"Yes, sir," said Henry. "We ran smack dab into that bunch of bandits."

"Where?" Cole said. "We're trailing them. They held up a coach, killed the messenger, and made off with the strong box."

"About eight miles south at an abandoned homestead surrounded by a limestone fence," Murphy said.

"That's the old Connelly place. They pulled stakes some years back after the fifth time the Indians raided their farm. Those men still headed south when you saw them?"

"They hit the end of the trail there, Sheriff," Murphy said. "You'll find their graves in back of the house. And you can find that Wells Fargo box, still locked tight, in the old root cellar nearby."

Cole's eyes widened. "You men killed all four? Every man Jack of them?"

"They were of a mind to rob us," Murphy said.

"And my companion and I don't cotton much to getting robbed," Henry added.

"Well, it seems you men saved us a sight of work," Cole said. "Where you headed?"

"We're freighting a load of flour up from San Antonio to Odessa," Henry lied smoothly.

Cole nodded. "You men stayin' in Odessa long? I might want to talk further with you later."

"A day or two, before we head back to San Antonio," Henry said.

"Much obliged," Cole said, touching his hat brim. Then he turned to his posse. "Let's go, men."

The posse galloped south and Murphy slapped the reins on the back of the team. "Giddy up now, you mules."

"Well, we did our civic duty, I guess," said Henry.

"I reckon we did."

# Chapter Twenty-Two

## Odessa

MURPHY AND HENRY ARRIVED at the outskirts of Odessa before dusk. But since they couldn't get to the bank until it opened the following day, they elected to stop and make a dry camp. If they had continued into town, they would have had to stay up all night guarding their cargo. Murphy figured they were safer staying outside the town until morning. So, Henry built a fire while Murphy watered the stock from the water barrel they had filled that morning from the well at the old Connelly place.

"It will be a relief to get your gold and silver inside the bank in the morning," Murphy said as they sat by the fire eating supper. "If that tale of Maximilian's treasure you told me was the truth, near thirty men have already died over your treasure. I sure didn't want our names added to the tally."

"Yep, I'll feel relieved, too."

"When you headed east?"

"I'm leaving on the first train out after I making the arrangements with the bank to send the money back to Maryland. How about you? You stayin' in Odessa for a spell?"

"Nope, I plan to ride west as soon as the money situation gets taken care of," Murphy said. "I've got a cattle drive to catch up with and someone to see."

"They headed to New Mexico Territory? Is that the plans you mentioned, young fella?"

"Yes, sir, that's it."

"Well, I'll be wishing you luck then, and I appreciate your help. Had I attempted this trip alone, those bandits we ran into would have been the end of my dreams."

Murphy nodded. "Hauling a fortune in gold and silver across the country is no job for the faint of heart. That's for sure."

AT NINE O'CLOCK THE next morning, Murphy stopped the team in front of the Odessa bank. Henry climbed down from the wagon and went inside to do his business. A little while later, he came outside with two bank employees and they moved the gold and silver inside the bank. An hour later, with arrangements made for the bank to wire Henry's money to a bank in Baltimore, Henry paid Murphy his five thousand in twenty-dollar U.S. government gold certificates. Murphy stuffed the notes into his saddlebags and then drove the team to the livery stable. There, Henry struck a deal with the livery owner and sold him the wagon and team. Murphy stabled the roan and accompanied the old prospector to the train depot. Henry bought a ticket but learned the next train east didn't depart until the following morning.

"If you would care to spend the night, I'll pay for your room at the hotel," Henry said.

After thinking it over, Murphy decided the least he could do was to see the old man safely on the train before leaving town. So, he accepted the offer. Knowing well the speed of a cattle drive, he reckoned delaying his journey west would put the herd no more than another twelve miles ahead of him than it already was. And a good night's sleep in an actual bed would do him good.

After stopping at a restaurant for a proper breakfast, the men booked rooms at the Ector House, the town's second-best hotel. After agreeing to meet for supper at six that evening, they parted. Murphy arranged for a bath and afterward retired to his room. Inside he found a narrow bed with a straw mattress, an old bureau, a white bowl and pitcher for washing, and on the floor a small section of rag rug.

Taking off his gun belt and boots with their run-down heels, he stretched out on the bed with a sigh. He was dog-tired after the trip from Comanche Gap and lonely. With the stress of shepherding Henry and his treasure to Odessa now behind him, all he could think of was Maria Espinosa and how badly he wanted to see her again. There was nothing to do but wait until morning. Then he would ride southwest out of town until he struck the Pecos and then follow it west until he overtook Maria and the herd. He reckoned the herd had probably made sixty or seventy miles since he'd left it, and hoped to overtake it in two days, long before Maria and her vaqueros crossed into New Mexico Territory.

Dressed in a clean outfit, Murphy met Henry in the hotel dining room for supper. There they enjoyed a sumptuous meal of steak, potatoes, and beans, the best grub Murphy believed he'd had in weeks. While they ate, Henry talked of Maryland, where he'd grown up in a town Murphy had spent time in during his youth during the War Between the States. After saying goodnight, they went back to their rooms to sleep.

———ele———

NEXT MORNING, MURPHY AGAIN met Henry in the dining room downstairs, this time for breakfast. Henry wore a new fancy suit of clothes he'd bought for his trip back east. After they finished the meal, Henry removed a worn, folded paper from the pocket inside his jacket.

For all you've done, young fella, I'm happy to offer you this map I bought from that doc. I've annotated it with notes that will help you identify all the landmarks. You could return to Comanche Gap and might find riches beyond your wildest dreams."

Murphy shook his head.

"Many thanks, but no thanks, old timer," Murphy said. "I've seen all of Comanche Gap I care to see, and I'm sure I've long since worn out my welcome there. And the way I see it, too much blood has already been spilled over that treasure."

Henry cackled and put the paper back in the inside pocket of his jacket.

"I guess I can't blame you, so I guess I'll hold on to the map as a souvenir."

Murphy walked with Henry to the train depot. There, they shook hands with the man before Henry boarded the train. After he had settled himself in a seat beside a window, Murphy waved his last goodbye to the eccentric old prospector as the train chugged out of the station. Then he walked to the livery to claim his horse. After paying the liveryman, he mounted the red roan and rode south out of town.

On the outskirts, he turned the horse to the southwest and rode across country. Anyone watching from the city would have soon seen the lone rider, sitting tall in the saddle, disappear from view into the heat waves wafting up from the parched earth of the Llano Estacado.

# Chapter Twenty-Three

## Fighting Words

THE SECOND DAY DAWNED. It was hot, dry, and brittle. The heat left a metallic taste in Murphy's mouth, and there was no wind. The sweat poured off him in the absence of any movement other than sitting his saddle as the roan plodded along at a walk. Yet he continued to ride across the trackless Llano Estacado without seeking shade, eager to catch the herd and see Maria once again.

At noon, Murphy struck the Pecos and found a shallow ford to cross over to the other side. The angled route he had taken southwest had saved him many miles. As he pointed the roan northwest, he followed the river toward the New Mexico Territory border. His practiced eyes, alert and watchful, surveyed the terrain. Soon he came across the churned earth and cow patties not yet dry that showed he was gaining on the thousand steers driven west by the vaqueros.

The life Ian Murphy had led had left him with few illusions. He was a man who had grown up facing danger, trouble, and hardship, knowing little else. But for the first time, he was acting with conscious, deliberate purpose. He was determined to buy his own little spread, build a comfortable home, run some good cattle, and raise fine horses.

More than anything, he hoped to build a life where he could put his gun away, a good life he also hoped Maria Espinosa would share with him. He marveled at the thought. Never had he met a woman until Maria that made him yearn for the things he now did. She had her own mind, and she had a temper, but Maria Espinosa was lots of other things, too. She was not merely pretty, but steady, loyal, and sincere. Not only had Murphy never met a woman like her, deep down inside he knew he'd never meet another like her. Such, he believed, did not exist. Not for him, at least.

The sun was low in the sky before Murphy saw the dust cloud ahead in the distance. He'd been smelling that dust for some time. He clapped his spurs to the roan, urging it from a walk to canter. Soon he could make out the vaqueros riding drag. A rider turned and rode toward him. Murphy had wondered if Maria would watch the back trail for him the way she had before. But then he felt disappointment when he recognized the approaching rider wasn't Maria, but Antonio, her segundo.

Murphy reined the roan to a stop when Antonio reached him. The man grabbed the saddlebags behind him and held them up.

"I've made a tally and am satisfied we have a thousand steers," Antonio said. "Inside these saddlebags is your money, fifteen dollars per head, as agreed. Take your money, Señor, and ride on. We do not wish you to join us."

"I'll be talking to Maria first, to see what she has to say about it," Murphy said evenly.

"I will not allow it, Señor. Don Pablo would not approve of you, and he would not welcome you at the rancho. Take your money and go, and we will avoid trouble."

"Antonio, I'm not going anywhere until I talk to Maria. And, if I have to, I'll cut a road through you to get to that herd to do it."

Antonio shook his head. "Take your money, Señor, and ride on before I become angry and decide to kill you."

"Try it, and I'll do the best I can to see that you don't," Murphy said.

Knowing Maria put great store by her segundo, Murphy wanted to end the dispute without gun play. So, he climbed off his horse and trailed the reins so the horse would stay put. Then he unbuckled his gun belt, threw it across his saddle, and took off his hat. After hanging the hat on the saddle horn, he turned back to Antonio.

"If we're going to quarrel, let's settle it like men with our fists, not guns."

Antonio's face was ugly with rage. "As you wish, Señor," he said. He climbed down from his horse, hung his sombrero on the saddle horn, and removed his gun belt. He swung the belt onto his saddle and then he rushed. His wicked right swing caught Murphy before he got his hands up, and it knocked him reeling into the dirt.

Antonio charged, his face livid, trying to put his boots to Murphy while he was down. But Murphy rolled away and sprang to his feet. Lunging, he swung a right of his own that clipped Antonio's left temple. Then he punched the vaquero on the point of the chin with a straight left. Then the men began slugging in earnest.

Both were raw, tough, hard-bitten men. They stood toe to toe, bloody and angry, and slugged it out. Antonio, as tall as but heavier than Murphy, confidently rushed in swinging. One of his punches opened a cut above Murphy's eye, and another started blood gushing from Murphy's nose. Antonio set himself and threw a hard straight right at Murphy's chin, but Murphy slipped the punch, and delivered a hard blow to Antonio's body that staggered him. The men came together again, and Murphy's big fist pulped Antonio's lips, knocking him back on his heels. Then Murphy waded in, throwing punches with his right and left, his breath coming in great gasps, but his gray eyes blazing. He charged in, following Antonio relentlessly, who seemed unable to ward off the blows. The big vaquero lowered his head and bull-rushed Murphy, driving a shoulder into Murphy's middle, putting him down in the dirt on his back. Antonio jumped astride him, and on his knees, sitting on Murphy's gut, he seized Murphy's neck with both hands and, after a few moments, darkness began washing over Murphy. Unable to breathe, he knew he'd soon go weak and helpless. He punched Antonio in the temple with his right and then his left again and again.

Suddenly, just as Murphy was about to lose consciousness, a gunshot rent the air.

"Stop it!" cried Maria Espinosa, leaping from her mount with her pistol in her hand. "Stop it now! What's going on here? Get off him, Antonio!"

Antonio staggered to his feet, wiping his bloody mouth with the back of his hand. Murphy rolled over onto his side, coughing and grasping for breath, and then he pushed himself up off the ground and stood up.

"Antonio, go back to the herd immediately! We shall speak about this later. Go now."

"Yes, *Jefe*," Antonio said sheepishly. Then he walked to his horse, strapped on his gun belt, put on his sombrero and then climbed on his horse. He wheeled the animal in a circle and clapped his spurs to the horse and rode away.

Murphy sank back down to the ground and sat gasping for air. Maria, with concern on her face, knelt beside him and wiped the blood off his face with a bandana.

"Are you hurt?" she said.

"I'm all right," Murphy said, "just a little winded."

"Why were you and Antonio fighting?"

"He rode out when he saw me coming," Murphy said. "He tried to pay me for the cattle and told me to take the money and ride on, that I wasn't welcome to join the herd."

"What! That's loco."

"Well, that's what he said, and I wasn't aiming to leave until I talked to you."

"Ian, for some reason, Antonio took it upon himself to do this. Of course, you're welcome to join us. I've looked for your return every day since you left us. I couldn't wait for you to come back to me."

Leaning forward, Maria wrapped her arms around Murphy and gently kissed his forehead. Then she burst out laughing.

"What's so funny?' Murphy said.

"I think Antonio has ruined your pretty face."

Murphy grinned. "Well, I guess he won't look so pretty in the morning, either."

Then they both laughed.

After he got his wind back, Murphy stood up and put his gun belt and hat back on. Then they both mounted their horses and rode toward the herd.

# Chapter Twenty-Four

## Distant Rumblings

WHEN MARIA AND IAN arrived back at the herd, Maria spurred his horse immediately over to Antonio, riding on a flank. Murphy held back, willing to let things with the segundo simmer down. But he saw from Maria's gesticulations she was giving Antonio a good dressing down. He sat on his horse, staring straight ahead, unwilling to meet her withering gaze. Then she turned her horse and rode back to Murphy and they rode side by side.

"There will be no further problems with Antonio," Maria said, still heated after the conversation with her segundo.

About an hour after Murphy had joined the herd, the vaqueros began bedding the cattle down for the night. After setting the first watch, the rest of the cowboys headed to the chuck wagon for supper. Later, they laid their bedrolls out around the campfire the cook had built to get some well-deserved sleep. This time, there was no handy stand of trees in the vicinity to provide a privacy screen, so Maria and Murphy laid out their bedrolls some distance away from the fire in the shadows, away from the rest of the crew.

Catching the scent of rain in the air, the last thing Murphy said before falling asleep was, "There's a storm brewin'." Then he drifted off to sleep thinking instead of breathing dust, the next morning they would slog through mud instead. What he and the outfit didn't know then was that morning would come a lot earlier to the cow camp than anyone expected.

IT WAS AFTER MIDNIGHT when the first fat, wet drops of rain hitting his face woke Murphy. Soon it became a driving rain. Maria and Ian grabbed their bedrolls and made for the wagon. There, they found slight shelter from the soaking rain. The cook had made his bed there as usual, but when the rain came, had squeezed into the wagon among the supplies, seeking a dry spot beneath the canvas. Along with the pelting rain came gusty winds and then Murphy saw the lightning strikes marching across the plains country from the southwest and heard the first distant rumblings of thunder.

Soon, laying in the slight shelter beneath the wagon, the pair heard Antonio shouting to his vaqueros to saddle their horses. An experienced cattleman, Antonio feared the same thing Murphy did. He and Maria crawled out from beneath the wagon, donned their slickers, and then grabbed their saddles before heading to the remuda with the rest of the crew.

Having ridden the red roan hard for two days to overtake the herd, Murphy threw his saddle onto a spare, rested horse. Just as he tightened the cinch, he heard the dreaded low rumbling noise and felt the earthquake-like tremors along the ground he'd experienced before too many times before. No one waited for the men of the watch guard to come in and give the alarm. Everyone in the crew already knew, and they all leaped on their saddled, jumping and snorting horses.

Driving cattle across country was a rough, hard, and dangerous business. Cattle drives were tough endeavors undertaken by tough men. Rustlers, hostile Indians, the risk of drowning while crossing swollen rivers, and pure accidents were all recognized hazards cowboys on a trail drive faced. But the hazard Murphy and other trail hands most feared were stampedes, and stampedes were common and most usually occurred at night.

The herd instinct in cattle was so great, the animals could go from a state of watchful relaxation to pandemonium in an instant. Lightning strikes, windy nights, a breaking stick in the darkness, or even a careless cowboy flaring a match to light a smoke could cause a stampede and the cattle would all bolt and run through the darkness in a mindless throng of hides and horns.

When a stampede happened, the cowboys had to mount their horses quickly and try to turn and mill the herd so they would not scatter to hell and back. Mounted on a horse running full tilt in the darkness after a herd of charging fear-crazed cattle was alone reason enough to consider stampedes the most notorious of all dangers on a cattle drive.

From the momentary light of the sporadic lightning flashes, Murphy saw the stampede was headed straight at the camp from where the vaqueros had bedded them down more than a mile away. It didn't surprise him as cattle most often stampeded back in the direction they had come from. The crew raced to intersect the onrushing avalanche of half-ton critters with Antonio,

Maria, and Murphy in the lead. Once they reached the rampaging steers, the crew rode alongside them some distance away while letting the cattle tire, which would make it easier to head them and get them into a mill. The means of halting a stampede was to turn the leaders to the right or left and getting them to run in a gradually smaller circle until they stopped.

After they passed back through the camp and run another six or seven miles, the herd had gone from a wedge-shaped mass to a line that strung out for over a mile with the faster most aggressive cattle leading and the slower, weaker animals running behind them. As the herd slowed, Murphy spurred his horse closer to the herd leaders and fired his Colt near the animal's ears.

Little by little, Murphy and the rest forced the leaders to turn to the right. As the herd swung right, they split in two, part of them turning left, making a circle of about two miles, with Murphy, Marie, and another vaquero heading that part of the herd. They kept running in a gradually smaller circle until they stopped. The other part of the herd kept on for a few miles further, then split into two groups, and Antonio and the other vaqueros divided and finally got both bunches stopped, but not until one bunch had gone about five miles beyond where Murphy, Maria, and the other rider had got the first bunch stopped and quieted. The storm had passed and now there was nothing more to be done until daylight, which would soon come.

# Chapter Twenty-Five

## Aftermath

AFTER COMBINING THE THREE bunches of cattle at first light, the vaqueros hazed the steers back up the trail, spending almost a full day getting them back where the stampede started. Miraculously, the herd hadn't overturned the wagon, although many of them had broken their horns on it and some their legs. The cook handed out cold biscuits, jerky, and coffee, a late lunch, to the arriving vaqueros before hitching his team and driving the wagon away towards the site where they would halt the herd that night.

Antonio sent three groups of three to four vaqueros to scour the countryside for strays before he and the rest of his men continued driving the main herd on to the northwest after the receding chuck wagon.

Murphy saw the carnage of the previous night around him. The worst of it was they came across the body of one vaquero. Apparently, his horse had stumbled or stepped into a hole and fallen in the stampede's path. There wasn't even any semblance of the rider left after those thousands of hoofs had got through pounding him beyond the tattered remnants of his clothing, which Marie used to identify as the young man named José

Luís, not yet twenty. He had been on his first cattle drive. Two vaqueros dug a hole with spades and buried what remained of José there and they left him alone in his lonesome, stone covered grave out on the vast prairie.

Some steers had died outright when they stumbled and fell and their fellows had trampled them into mincemeat. Those still alive but down with broken legs, the vaqueros shot. Hundreds had their broken off horns hanging only by slivers.

After they finished their coffee and modest lunch, Maria told Murphy they would ride ahead of the herd after the chuck wagon, so she could select the night's campsite. As Murphy moved his saddle from the borrowed pony to his roan, a heavy hand clapped him on the shoulder. He turned to face Antonio.

"Muchas Gracias, Señor," Antonio said stiffly, offering his hand. "You helped us save the herd."

Murphy nodded and they shook hands.

"Adios," the big man said, and then he turned and walked to his horse, mounted, and rode away.

Murphy reckoned it unlikely he and Antonio would ever become friends, but at least it seemed the fight and Murphy's skills as a cowboy had at least earned the man's grudging respect.

After they made camp for the night, Antonio reported to Maria that he estimated they had lost fifty steers to the stampede, including those trampled and the cripples the vaqueros had to shoot. Murphy knew it could have been far worse. More vaqueros might have died than the one young man, as regrettable as his loss was. Murphy just felt relieved that Maria hadn't suffered harm. But perhaps that hadn't surprise him much as she seemed as skilled and tough as her vaqueros.

The grass was fine, and water for the cattle was plentiful. The herd covered another twenty miles and crossed the New Mexico Territory line without further mishap. Sunny, cloudless days and bright moonlit nights prevailed. In another four or five days, if their luck held, they would arrive at Fort Sumner.

# Chapter Twenty-Six

## Fort Sumner

AT THE END OF the week, on Friday afternoon, Maria and Antonio halted the herd outside the town in sight of the stone walls of Fort Sumner at Bosque Redondo, the army post established to protect the adjacent Indian reservation where the government had interned the Navajo and Apache. Maria sent her segundo to the fort to arrange the transfer of the cattle. About an hour later, a cavalry detachment commanded by a young lieutenant and the Indian agent, a civilian the government appointed to supervise the reservation, rode out to the herd. The agent accepted the delivery of the herd after Maria explained the loss of the fifty head of cattle to the stampede.

"That's acceptable," the agent said. "The contract guaranteed delivery of a minimum of nine hundred steers and you've fulfilled that. Please convey my respects to your father, Don Pablo. The government will remit payment to his bank, per our standing arrangements."

"Thank you, Señor Johnson," Maria said.

The soldiers took over to drive the herd to the government's grazing land. The chuck wagon had already left for the rancho, and Antonio had not returned. Maria assumed he had gone on to the rancho after arranging with Johnson and the army to accept the delivery of the steers. So Murphy rode with Maria and the rest of her vaqueros to the rancho.

"You can stay at the house as our guest until we have an opportunity to speak with my father about selling you the land," Maria said. "I wired him from Comanche Gap about the difficulties with Señor Logan and mentioned your name as the man who helped resolve our problem. But I want my father to spend some time with you to get acquainted."

"I'm happy to meet your father," Murphy said. "But I don't wish to impose on your father's hospitality. I'll see you to the rancho and say howdy, but I'll get a room at the hotel in town."

"Oh, no you won't," said Maria with a chuckle. "I insist you stay with us at the rancho."

When they arrived, the size of the hacienda impressed Murphy. Rancho de Don Pablo looked like a first class operation. The vaqueros split off toward the bunkhouse as Maria and Murphy rode into the yard. They tied their horses to the hitch rack out front, and the front door opened. A gray-haired gentleman of medium height with a bushy mustache and wearing a brown short leather vaquero jacket and brown pants with silver conchos lining the outside seams stepped out, followed by Antonio.

The older man crossed the veranda and descended the steps, while Antonio remained on the wide porch, leaning against a post with his thumbs tucked inside his gun belt.

"Papa!" cried Maria, throwing her arms around the man's neck.

Don Pablo placed his hands on her shoulders and gently pushed her away.

"Welcome home, daughter," he said, and then turned to look at Murphy.

"Papa, may I present Señor Ian Murphy," Maria said. "I mentioned him in the wire I sent you. Ian agreed to sell us the needed cattle after I learned that Señor Logan tried to sell us stolen cattle."

Don Pablo nodded, but neither smiled nor extended a hand in greeting.

"Please go into the house, Maria," said Don Pablo. "You must be tired after your journey. I will speak with Señor Murphy alone."

Maria looked at her father quizzically, having noticed his lack of friendliness toward Ian.

"That won't be necessary," Maria said. "I'm not tired, and Ian will stay with us for a few days. We—"

"Maria Espinosa Díaz!" Don Pablo cried, interrupting her. "Do as I say. Go inside, now. We will speak later."

While she was a grown woman, Maria had recognized since her childhood the tone her father used when he intended to brook neither argument nor discussion. She cast an apologetic look at Murphy, but then, her eyes blazing with anger, she stomped up the steps and into the house, slamming the front door behind her.

"Thank you for your assistance, Señor Murphy," Don Pablo said formally. "Have you received payment for the cattle?"

"No, sir, but I haven't asked for it. If it wouldn't be an inconvenience, I'd like to give you the name and information of my boss back in Texas and have you transfer the money through your bank to his."

"Very well. When we've finished our talk, please give the information to Antonio and I will do as you ask."

"Thank you."

"Now, with our business concluded, please leave my rancho and do not return."

Don Pablo's unexpected words felt like a slap in the face to Murphy. He had realized the man hadn't seemed friendly, but he hadn't expected Don Pablo to order him off the place.

"With all due respect, I reckon your daughter might have something to say about that," Murphy said, suddenly angry.

"When I ask you for an opinion," said Don Pablo indignantly. "Such a remark might be in order. Until then, you may keep your remarks to yourself."

"Sir, I don't wish to quarrel with you," Murphy said. "I love your daughter and I'd like her to become my wife if she'll have me."

"Impossible!" Don Pedro cried angrily. "You will stay away from my daughter. Do you hear? Unless you wish for trouble. Antonio has brought me a full report, and you are not the right sort of man for Maria. I would never consent to her marrying a common gunman, a killer like you. Never. Now leave my rancho. Do not return."

Don Pedro turned on his heel, mounted the steps, and went into the house. Antonio descended the steps. Instead of a look of satisfaction on his face, Murphy thought Antonio appeared apologetic.

"I'm sorry, Señor," he said. "But my loyalty belongs to Don Pedro. He has employed me since I was a boy.

Please give me the instructions and I will ensure we send the payment for the cattle without delay to your boss in Texas."

Murphy knew he couldn't fault Antonio for doing what he believed his boss, Don Pedro, expected. Taking out his tally book, Murphy scribbled Colonel Ward's name and his Fort Stockton bank name on a slip of paper. Tearing it out of the book, he handed it to Antonio.

"Now, you must leave the rancho," Antonio said almost kindly as he took the offered slip of paper.

"I'd be obliged, Antonio, if you would kindly get word to Maria that I'll be at the hotel in town when she can see me."

Antonio nodded, but it seemed more a gesture to acknowledge he'd heard what Murphy said than any commitment to do what he had asked. Murphy walked to his horse, mounted the roan, and rode out of the yard towards Fort Sumner.

# Chapter Twenty-Seven

## Disillusioned

MURPHY RODE TOWARD TOWN, still astonished by Don Pablo's rancorous attitude towards him. He understood how a father might believe a man wasn't good enough for his daughter. But the man had been offensively impolite. And he had acted as if Maria, a grown woman, had no right to make her own choices. Truly, Murphy hadn't expected Don Pablo to accept him into the family with open arms immediately. Maybe he was a traditional sort who expected his daughter to choose someone from her own culture, perhaps someone like Antonio, not an Anglo as her beau. But Murphy had believed if given a chance, he could have won Maria's father over. Yet there would be no chance. Don Pablo had ordered him off the place and warned him not to return. He'd even threatened him, not the sort of rude behavior Murphy was in a habit of tolerating from any man. Yet he couldn't very well fight Maria's father, or even Antonio for that matter, without damaging his fledgling relationship with Maria. Finally, Murphy convinced himself he'd have to trust Maria. He felt sure she'd come to him as soon as she could. Maybe she'd persuade her father to give him a chance. Together, he and Maria would find a solution. He reckoned Maria would prefer to get her father's blessing, but he couldn't imagine she wouldn't defy him if there was no alternative. For Murphy knew he loved Maria, and he believed firmly that she felt the same about him.

When he arrived in town, Murphy made his first stop at the telegraph office. Back in Comanche Gap, he'd already posted a letter through the stage line mail to Colonel Ward telling him of his son's death and that he had delivered justice to those responsible. He had also reported that he had recovered the stolen cattle from the rustlers and was selling them to an interested buyer on Ward's behalf, so they didn't have to drive the steers back to Fort Stockton. So, in the telegram, Murphy simply told Ward the buyer would transfer the proceeds from the cattle sale to his bank and informed him he wouldn't be returning to Fort Stockton.

While buying land from Maria's father no longer looked promising, Murphy still intended to remain in New Mexico Territory. He figured he could ask around town until he located some range land with good grass and water where he could establish the ranch he dreamed of building.

Ian took a room at the town's only hotel, telling the clerk he wasn't sure how long he'd be staying and would pay by the day. Then he ordered up a bath and washed the trail dust off. Afterwards, he got a good meal and then went to his room to sleep.

AFTER WATCHING MURPHY RIDE away from the parlor window, Maria went to her father's study to confront him. But Don Pablo cut her off immediately.

"I forbid you to see that man again, and do not challenge me," her father said. Choose a decent man from our culture to marry and bear me grandchildren I can be proud of."

After forbidding her to see Murphy again if she intended to take over the rancho someday at his passing, he told her he wished to hear nothing more about Murphy. When she tried to argue, he ordered her to go to her room.

Upset, Maria went upstairs to her room, threw herself on the bed and tearfully considered her options. She had never seen her father act so unreasonably. He hadn't even allowed her to speak. It was if her feelings didn't matter. She believed her father was a good man, and he had always treated her well. But if he refused to even listen to her, she knew in her heart she would defy him whether or not her father disinherited her. If that was his decision, so be it.

Maria decided after dark came, she would saddle her horse and ride to town to see Ian. But then she heard a key in the lock of her door. Springing from the bed, she hurried to the door and found her father had locked it. She pounded on the door with her fists and screamed his name until she became hoarse. Then she collapsed to the floor next to the door in disbelief and wept. Her father had imprisoned her in her own home and there was no escape. How would she get to Ian now?

On Saturday, Murphy visited the saloons in town, not because he wanted to drink but because saloons were clearinghouses for local information in all western towns. In the saloons, he talked to local cowboys, bought a few drinks, and learned of several properties the owners were looking to sell.

Leaving the last saloon, Murphy turned into a restaurant for his noontime meal. He studied the menu, pleased to see there were more options on offer than was usual for a western town. When the door opened, Murphy looked up from the menu to see a square-shouldered man of medium height enter. The man's eyes roved over the room and then settled on Murphy, who saw a silver star pinned to man's vest. The lawman walked to Murphy's table.

"New in town?" the sheriff asked.

"Yes, sir, I came in with a herd Friday," Murphy said.

The lawman nodded. "Plan on staying in Fort Sumner for a spell?"

"Yes, permanent like, maybe."

Murphy knew local lawmen always took an interest in strangers arriving in their towns. They wanted to take the measure of such men to get ahead of potential troublemakers. So Ian took no offense at the sheriff's interest. The lawman looked him over again, more carefully.

"This is good country, and we can always use good men," he said. "Planning on ranching?"

"In a small way. The name is Murphy, Sheriff. I'm looking to buy some range land hereabouts to build a little ranch and raise a few cows."

"Do tell," the lawman said. "Found any property yet that interests you?"

"I've heard rumors about some properties up for sale I might be interested in looking over," Ian said. "Sit down, Sheriff. I'd be interested to learn what you know about the owners of the properties I've heard about and how I might contact them."

"Thanks." The sheriff dropped into the chair across from Murphy. The waitress came over and put a cup of coffee and a menu in front of him and topped off Murphy's cup. "My name's Ted Gee. Whenever a stranger wearing a tied down gun comes into town, I try to make his acquaintance."

Murphy nodded. "Sounds like a solid policy to keep the peace in your town."

Gee grinned, more cordial now, but his eyes remained curious and alert.

"What properties have you heard about?"

"I've got a list here," Murphy said, digging his tally book out of his shirt pocket. He opened the book and read from the notes he'd written while talking to cowmen at the saloons earlier.

Gee nodded. "Yes, I understand all those men are looking to sell. You know anybody in town?" he asked.

"Only the people out at the Don Pablo Díaz rancho. I sold them some steers over in Texas and trailed along with them to Fort Sumner."

Ted Gee looked again at the tall man across the table, measuring him and wondering.

"Don Pablo rarely involves himself with the Anglos hereabouts," Gee said. "He pretty much keeps to himself out on his big hacienda. And he keeps his vaqueros in line and I've never had trouble with a single one of them when they come into town. He runs the biggest spread around these parts. It sets on the biggest Spanish land grant in the territory and has been in his family for three generations. Out of curiosity, how did you meet Don Pedro?"

"I only met him for the first time Friday afternoon when we got in to Fort Sumner with the herd," Murphy said. "My acquaintance is more with his daughter, Maria. And I can't claim Don Pablo found me all that impressive."

Gee grinned again. "Reckoned you knew her, and imagine I can figure that one out. No offense, but I expect a man like you, an Anglo I mean, isn't exactly the kind of man he intends to win the hand of his only daughter."

"That was sort of my impression, too."

The waitress brought the plates of food they had ordered and put it on the table before them. The men ate silently for a while.

"You've seen my gun, Sheriff, and probably recognized I've been over the trail a time or two. But let me put your mind at ease. I'm only in town looking for land to build a home and run a few cows. Mostly, I want to be left alone and intend to accord others the same courtesy. I've never been drunk in my life and will be in town only occasionally when I need supplies. You'll have no trouble with me."

Gee nodded thoughtfully. "Fair enough," he said. Then he told Murphy what he knew about the property owners on his list and told him where he could find them.

In the evening, after having supper, Murphy went back to his room to think. He reckoned he'd make informal visits on Sunday to the properties he'd gathered information on to see whether any seemed suitable for his purposes. But he would wait until Monday to contact the owners of any properties he found interesting. He expected Maria to come to see him by Sunday at the latest, and he wanted her opinions on any property he considered before buying.

ON SUNDAY, MURPHY RODE around the country and looked at four properties. One had little water access for watering stock, so he scratched it from the list. Another didn't offer good grass, and he discounted that property, too. But the other two seemed definite possibilities. One had an old rundown house on it, which he could use temporarily until he was ready to build his own ranch house. The fourth property he liked best as far as the grass and water availability, but it was bare range land and would require him to build immediately.

Late Sunday evening, when Maria had still come looking for him or sent word, Murphy began to worry. Even if Antonio hadn't passed on his message, wouldn't she assume he was at the hotel, the only one in the town? Maybe she didn't care for him as much as she had let on, or maybe her father had threatened to disown or disinherit her if she defied him. Having seen the place, Murphy knew it would be a tough choice for Maria or anyone to turn their back on such an impressive estate.

As Don Pablo's only child, Maria stood to inherit it all. Don Pablo had impressed Murphy as a man ornery enough to threaten to disinherit his own daughter if she acted in opposition to his wishes. Murphy went to sleep on Sunday night feeling disheartened and lonely.

# Chapter Twenty-Eight

## Change of Heart

ON MONDAY, MURPHY VISITED the owners of the two properties that interested him and found both men cordial. The price set on the property with the tumbledown house seemed about right, but the man selling the bare range land set a price Murphy found a little high. He reckoned he might negotiate the price down a little closer to reasonable if he decided he wanted to buy that tract of land. After telling both owners he'd be back once he decided about making an offer, Murphy rode back to town.

When he inquired at the hotel, the clerk told him no one had called for him and there were no messages. That was when the hurt Murphy felt from Maria making no effort to contact him turned toward resentment. He began wondering who he thought he was fooling. Certainly not himself. It was also when he acknowledged that the only reason he had considered settling down in Fort Sumner had been Maria, and without that, there was nothing about the country he found particularly appealing. He had considered moving from Texas in the past to some place folks hadn't heard of Ian Murphy. A place where his name wouldn't work against him and he could put his gun away permanently and people would let him alone. But until he met Maria Espinosa, New Mexico Territory had never been on his list of possibilities.

Later, lying in bed trying to quiet his troubled mind, Murphy reached a decision. He had considered riding back to Don Pablo's rancho and demanding to speak to Maria. If her father had convinced her or coerced her into forgetting having a life with him, Murphy wanted to hear it from her. But he knew doing that could end, probably would end in violence. While Murphy had no fear of that, he realized it wouldn't solve his dilemma. So in the end, the decision he reached was he'd give Maria until noon the next day to come to him, or at least send word to show she remained interested. If neither happened, then he would pack his kit and haul his freight out of Fort Sumner. The money he'd earned from Charlie Henry would spend just as well somewhere else as in New Mexico Territory. Maybe he'd head for the cattle country of Montana where he'd heard there was forty million acres of rich grazing land with some of the best grasses in the West.

TUESDAY NOON CAME AND went with no word from Maria Espinosa. Heartbroken, but with resentment now in full flame, Murphy paid his bill at the front desk and carried his saddlebags from the hotel to the livery. There, he saddled the roan and climbed aboard and tipped his hat to the stableman.

"Where you headed?" the stableman asked, noticing Murphy seemed set for travel.

Ian said nothing, but with a wry grin pointed north. Then the lone rider on the long-legged roan left Fort Sumner. He was a gray-eyed man wearing a black high-crowned, wide-brimmed hat, a cotton shirt under a brown leather vest, and brown wool pants. He was riding easy as the people of the town watched him ride north out of town toward Colorado.

⁂

ANTONIO RODE INTO THE rancho yard and tied his horse at the hitch rack in front of the large house. Mounting the steps, he crossed the wide porch and let himself in through the front door. His big-roweled spurs jingled as he walked down the hallway to Don Pedro's study. There he found the man sitting behind his ornate wooden desk, shuffling papers. He looked up when Antonio walked in.

"The gringo rode out of town yesterday," Antonio said. "I found no one in town that he told where he was going. She cannot find him."

Don Pedro nodded. "Bueno."

Antonio turned and left the room. Don Pedro stood and ran a hand through his gray hair. Someday, he believed Maria would understand he had done what he believed in her best interests. Life would go on and she would forget Ian Murphy in time.

He took stairs up. Pausing at her door, he produced a key from his pocket. He inserted it, turned the lock, and opened the door. He found his daughter sitting up on the edge of the bed as if she had just awakened.

"What?" she demanded with undisguised contempt and anger.

"The man has gone away," Don Pedro said. "Now you can forget him and choose a proper man from our culture as your husband."

"And provide you with the grandchildren you can take pride in that you spoke of?" Maria said with sarcasm.

Standing, she crossed the room and, with eyes flashing, slapped her father's face.

"Thanks to you, Papa, your grandchild I now carry may never know his or her father. You must be proud."

Don Pedro stood open-mouthed, gaping at her words, barely registering his daughter had dared to slap him.

Pushing past him, Maria bolted downstairs, out the front door, and ran to the stable. There she saddled her horse quickly, spurred the horse out of the rancho yard and rode toward town at a gallop.

Maria rode first to the hotel. She tied the horse and hurried inside.

"Yes, ma'am?" the clerk said.

"Has Ian Murphy checked out?" Maria asked breathlessly.

"Yes, ma'am, he left around noon yesterday."

"I am Maria Espinosa Díaz," she said. "Did he leave a message for me?"

"No, ma'am, he left no messages."

"Did he mention where he was going?"

"No, he seemed a man who kept to himself. He hardly spoke two words to me the whole time he was here."

"Thank you," Maria said before hurrying out and almost colliding with Sheriff Gee."

"I expect you're looking for Murphy," the lawman said. "You're a little late, ma'am. He rode out of town yesterday."

"You spoke to him?"

"I sure did," Gee said, taking off his hat and scratching his head before settling the hat back in place. "It surprised me when I heard he left. He told me he was looking for land to build a ranch."

"He mentioned nothing about where he might have gone?"

"No, ma'am. As I said, I hadn't expected he was leaving at all."

"Thank you, Sheriff," Maria said. Then she turned and hurried on foot towards the livery, tears already welling in her dark eyes.

At the livery stable, Maria received only more heart-breaking news.

"No, ma'am," he didn't say," the liveryman said, leaning on his pitchfork. "I even asked and all he did was point to the north. Colorado maybe? Though it's hard to tell. There is plenty of country north of Colorado, too."

Grieving, her eyes now filled with tears, Maria stumbled back to the hotel in a daze and mounted her horse. Had Ian not truly cared for at all? Hadn't he known she would have come to him if her father hadn't prevented her? Yet he hadn't even bothered to leave a note. At the edge of town, she broke down, leaned forward in the saddle and sobbed openly as the horse carried her back toward the rancho. How would she ever find him now to tell him of the child she had expected them to raise together?

# Chapter Twenty-Nine

## Home

SIX WEEKS AFTER LEAVING New Mexico Territory, having crossed Colorado and Wyoming, Murphy arrived in Montana in late August. When he first arrived, the sight that immediately impressed him was the beautiful stretches of grass waving in the breeze like vast fields of grain. He saw blue grama, buffalo grass, needle-and-thread grass, western wheat grass, and other native species. He also noted the abundant stream beds that threaded through Montana, providing both water and shelter for ranging cattle.

Over the weeks of travel, Murphy's heart had gradually hardened and the pain he'd left behind had lessened. He had accepted Maria Espinosa, whatever her reason, had changed her mind about him. Of course, Murphy had no way of knowing how wrong he was.

Back in Fort Sumner, after returning to the rancho, Maria never again spoke a single word to her father, Don Pedro. Though the man lived, she treated him as though he were dead to her. She spent most of her time alone, inside her bedroom, with the door locked. Maria no longer took part in the operations of the rancho. She had lost all interest in it. Many times, her father and Antonio had tried to talk with her, reason with her, but she paid them no mind and simply walked away. Murphy knew none of that, nor about the child growing within the woman he had loved. He rarely even thought of her any longer.

To the high valleys of Montana rode the lone rider, a man who felt at home in untamed lands restless with danger. The Indian Wars were largely in the past, with the Blackfeet, Gros Ventre, Sioux, Crow, and Northern Cheyenne confined to reservations. Cattle had replaced the Buffalo, and bold men had pushed their herds into the valleys lush with grass where cattle fattened amazingly fast.

It was into one such valley Murphy rode. He drew up and looked around him. Then he decided. This was the home he had looked for. On this land, he would stay. Turning in his saddle, he looked around the valley he had found. It looked to be over two thousand acres, lush with grass, and there was water aplenty. Yes, here in this lonesome place, he would stop. He would cease being the drifter trying to escape his reputation as a gunman, a killer. Here in this place, he would stay and find peace.

# About Author

**RUSTY BEAUQUET** is the pen name of a published American multi-genre writer of fiction, best known for his mystery & detective and police procedural novels. Beauquet, a retired Texas peace officer, grew up in Oklahoma and has lived much of his adult life in Texas. *The Reckoning*, the debut book in the new Lone Rider classic western series, is his first western novel. Rusty is an avid, lifelong fan of Louis L'Amour and Zane Grey and enjoys reading many of the other great writers of western fiction.

Visit https://rustybeauquet.com to learn more.

# Also By Rusty Beauquet

The Reckoning, Lone Rider #1
Comanche Gap, Lone Rider #2

**Coming Soon**

The Rock Creek Valley War, Lone Rider #3

www.ingramcontent.com/pod-product-compliance
Lightning Source LLC
Chambersburg PA
CBHW021448150726
47989CB00001B/444